Run To Me

ASHLYNN MILLS

Warnings

Stepbrothers, adopted brothers, murder, self-harm, childhood trauma, mentioning of trafficking, push and pull. Separation between MCs, mentions of child abuse, kidnapping (not between MCs) and cheating (not between MCs).

Copyright©2025 @Ashlynn Mills

All rights reserved.

No part of this book may be reproduced, scanned, or distributed in any oriented or electronic form without permission.

This is a work of fiction. Names and characters have been made up, and the story came from the author's imagination. Any resemblance to real life events or people is pure coincidence.

Cover design: Charli Childs

Betas: Courtnay Gray, and Tammy Jones.

Editor: SJ Buckley

Thank you to my team for always being so amazing!

Contents

Prologue	1
One	6
Two	13
Three	20
Four	29
Five	36
Six	52
Seven	60
Eight	65
Nine	73
Ten	81
Eleven	92
Twelve	100
Thirteen	110

Fourteen	114
Fifteen	121
Sixteen	127
Seventeen	129
Eighteen	136
Nineteen	138
Twenty	140
Twenty-One	149
Twenty-Two	156
Twenty-Three	160
Twenty-Four	172
Twenty-Five	179
Twenty-Six	186
Twenty-Seven	194
Twenty-Eight	202
Twenty-Eight	205
Twenty-Nine	207
Thirty	209
Thirty-One	215
Thirty-Two	219
Thirty-Three	223
Thirty-Four	225
Thirty-Five	230
Thirty-Six	233

Thirty-Seven	236
Epilogue	238
Athor's note	240

Prologue

JACE

Eleven years old

I open my eyes to a dark room smelling of Clorox and metal. Silence surrounds me and there's not so much as a creaking floorboard. No loud breathing from anyone but me either. Does that mean he's dead? I'm not usually this sloppy, but I lost focus after looking up at my mom and seeing pictures of her new family. She was in one of her sun dresses, standing between who I assume to be her husband and his son. My dad was right, her intentions were always to replace us. Not only didn't she want him anymore, but she didn't want me either. So many days I would lie in bed, wishing she'd fought harder to take me with her. That was seven years ago. I have to learn to forget her. If only it was that easy.

My head aches and I sway a little trying to get to my feet. I feel around me, guiding myself toward the steps. I forgot to lock the door behind me and my father's new guest got out while I was dozing on the couch. I wouldn't have heard him if he hadn't crashed into the standing lamp nearby. Scared and shaking, he'd tried to run but I was faster.

He put up quite the fight too, when I finally caught up to him. He kicked and screamed, his arms flailing everywhere. "Please," he begged, sounding weak and tired.

"I'm sorry but you have to go back to the basement or we'll both be in trouble." An impending fear crept up my back, feeling like a million ants were crawling on my skin. Last time I made a mistake I paid big time for it, and was locked up in the basement shelter room for days without food and only a dog bowl filled with water. I can't go back there again so soon. So I did everything I could to get the guy back in the basement, ignoring the dread tugging at my insides.

He can't be older than twenty, with blond hair and a dusting of freckles over his nose. Skinny and frail, he was stronger than he looked, but so was I. Many people call me big for my age, assuming I'm at least four years older than I am. "I'm sorry," I kept saying as I dragged him down the steps. His nails clawed at the walls, and he managed to latch on so well that I lost balance and we both fell down the steps. He was so heavy. Maybe he's only passed out like I was.

The throbbing in my head continues, and when I rub my temple my fingers come in contact with something wet and sticky. Either way, my dad's going to know something went wrong. I'm getting punished for this, but it's my fault for not following the rules. For letting my guard down. It's my fault we're both hurt and going to suffer more than we already have. It's all my fault.

Hiding under my bed or in the closet won't help me. He always finds me no matter where I go. I like to pretend I'm safe when I bury myself under the sea of clothes in the back anyway, and it does give me extra time to disappear into my own head before the pain comes.

Eyes watering, my hands shake as I flip on the light switch, and I hold on to the railing when a dizzy spell comes over me. I make my way slowly up the stairs and stop on the second step, and when I turn around my heart squeezes. A body lies on the floor of the basement in a fetal position, not moving. Fuck. Fuck. The difference between me and my dad is, I don't hurt them, but I fear the day he finally trains me to take over doing what needs to be done to protect our home. To protect us. Instead, I help him keep them fed and clean, and I treat their wounds. I also watch over them while he's at work, making sure they remain in the basement and don't hurt themselves.

"Don't worry, son," he'd say. *"This is only to help prepare them for their new homes. Life will be better for them once they're there. You should be proud to have helped them get there."*

Chills run up and down my body. "Hey," I whisper, tapping the guy's leg with my foot when I'm close enough. He's in nothing but a pair of gray sweats my dad keeps for all our visitors, half of his blond strands covered in blood. "Hey," I say again, my voice shaking. "I need you to wake up. Please wake up." I drop to my knees, checking for a pulse, and sigh in relief when I finally get one. Sweat gathers on my forehead as I flip him over onto his back.

His eyes slowly blink and then quickly widen when they land on me. "No," he screams, glancing around the room frantically. "I can't be down here again. Please don't make me. I'll do anything you want, just don't leave me here." Turning toward me, he clings to my leg, and I push him away. He tries to sit up and immediately crashes to his knees.

"I have to. I wish I didn't. I really wish there was another way," I say, and my throat tightens around each word. My phone buzzes in my pocket and it's my dad saying he'll be home late. Another message quickly follows, leaving me more tense than before.

Dad: There better not be a mess for me to clean up when I get home.

Swallowing hard, I exit the message and my fingers linger over the keys, struggling to press down on the right numbers.

"I think I need a hospital," the guy grits out. "I hit my head pretty bad and I feel sick."

"I got the first aid kit and some water." My words rush out as I back up against the steps. I shouldn't have to tie him up again with the state he's in.

"That's not good enough. I need a fucking doctor. Are you a doctor?"

I shake my head, words trapped in my throat.

"Why are you doing this?" His face twists.

"My dad said we have to."

"You don't, though. You can still help me, you know. You can still do the right thing," he croaks.

"But this is the right thing." I wasn't so sure anymore. My head has been such a messed up place lately and I've been constantly at war with myself. Why would my dad do this if he really didn't have to?

His eyes blink hard and his face pales. "Oh my God. You're just a child. Why didn't I notice before? How old are you?"

"I'm not supposed to be talking to you."

"You don't like doing this, do you? Does he hurt you too?" He crawls toward me, his eyes struggling to stay open.

"I have to get you cleaned up. I'll be right back."

"No," he shouts and I run up the steps as fast as I can. His screams are muffled when I close the door and I press my back to it, taking deep breaths. I eye the burn scars on my arms and remind myself to keep doing what I've been instructed to do. Dad will be home soon and I won't have to deal with it anymore. Not until he leaves again. I squeeze my eyes shut, tears hitting my cheeks. The guy downstairs was right. I don't want to do this. I never did.

After locking the door, I go to the bathroom to get towels, the first aid kit, and medical tape. I grab Tylenol from my dad's room on the way back to the basement, and find the man flipped onto his back with his body convulsing. *Shit*. That can't be good. None of this is good. Dropping everything to the ground, I leave the basement and rush out the front door, needing air. I can't breathe. My knees crash to the ground, pants soaking from the wet grass as I tug at the collar of my shirt.

"What's wrong, son?" A deep voice comes from beside me but my world is spinning too fast to know from where. I fall forward, wrapping my hands around myself, rocking, and the tears fall faster than before as I hyperventilate. A large weight lands on my back and voices grow louder around me.

Someone says something about calling for help, and that's when a deep panic rests heavily on my chest. "No," I scream, curling into a ball on the grass.

"It's okay, son. We're calling for help. They'll be here soon."

"Fuck. His head is bleeding. Who did that to you, kid?" another voice says.

"Tell my dad I can't do it anymore." I rasp out a breath, my head feeling light and heavy all at once. "I can't. I'm sorry. I'll take my punishment in the storm room for however long I have to. Just tell him not to make me do it anymore."

"Do what?" A man looks down at me with furrowed brows.

"Be like him," I say before my whole world goes black.

One

JACE

Fifteen years old

The kitchen goes from being filled with laughter and light conversation to quiet when I enter. Years of therapy and spending time in group homes have done nothing to help me feel like I belong any more than I did the first time my mom came to get me from the hospital. I remember the distraught look in her eyes as she reached for me. She was looking for me for a while. My dad picked me up from daycare one day without her knowing and went off the map. I was never supposed to end up with him, but he didn't take too kindly to my mom gaining full custody. She held me for hours when finally getting me back, promising to never leave me again, and then she did when I wasn't acting normal enough for her. I didn't eat more than once a day, hardly spoke, locked myself in my room, and slept in the closet. To them it was something to worry about, but for me it was what I'd become accustomed to. All I was doing was following the rules. Before, I got in trouble for breaking them, and now I get punished when I abide by them.

"Morning, hun," my mom says, with a smile on her face. "How'd you sleep?"

"Good enough." I shrug and sit in the empty chair, inhaling the delicious scent of pancakes on the table.

"Are you taking the bus to school today, or did you want me to give you a ride?" Terry asks. He keeps wanting me to refer to him as dad, but doesn't seem to understand how detached to the word I've become. I'm also struggling to find a connection here. Calling someone mom every day is already almost too much for me to handle.

"The bus is fine." I reach for my fork, shifting in my seat.

"Are you sure you're ready? You don't have to rush it." My mom's eyes fill with worry, and my stepbrother Nate has barely said a word to me ever since I moved back in three weeks ago. He just stares like I'm some new breed at the zoo he's trying to figure out. He's either scared of me, or doesn't like having to adjust to me being here. Maybe both. I'd made a mistake on my second day back. I meant well. It had helped the others. They thanked me for it too, sometimes.

Nate had looked like he was having trouble sleeping, so I crushed up some of my sleeping meds and put them in his water bottle when he wasn't looking. I only wanted to help. Why can't I stop doing the wrong thing? What does that even mean anymore? Years later and my brain is still somewhere trapped between bad and good, unable to fully differentiate the two. Will I ever get it right? Will I ever belong here? My stomach feels as if a boulder has landed inside it.

"I'm sure. I miss school—regular school," I finally respond. I do too. School at the group home wasn't the same. I was shoved into classes with kids either way younger or older and the staff were often leery around me. They were better company than my dad was at least, giving me room to learn from my mistakes instead of beating me every time I get something wrong. And the adults there smiled a lot more. Much like my mom is doing now. I both prefer it and hate it. Why give me those now when I needed them more before?

My mom rests a hand on mine. "Okay. But if you need me to come get you at any time—"

"I'll call you. I have everyone's number saved on my phone." My mom got me a new one for when I was away from home, so she could call me every day. She mostly talked while I listened, and I nodded like she could see me, but she never brought up the day I'd let my dad down. It's taken a while for me to come to terms with the fact that he was the one who messed up, not me. What we were doing wasn't for the good of anything or anyone except him and the sex-trafficking ring he got himself wrapped up in. He told the cops they'd come after me if he stopped providing what they agreed upon, but I doubt that's the main reason he kept at it.

My dad liked the fancy life—nice cars and our big house in a quiet neighborhood. He was too lost in his own dreams to care about anything else, and I was too scared to believe anything other than what he was telling me. Scared and loyal. As kids, we only have our parents to rely on. To teach us and guide us. I don't know what I'm supposed to be doing half the time. Everything I learned to be from my dad has been ingrained in me, and it'll take a lot longer than a few years to unlearn.

We finish eating in silence. They can't be their full selves around me, and I don't even know how I'm supposed to be, or who they want me to be. That's why I don't do anything but eat until it's time to leave for school. Nate steps up onto the bus behind me, walking past me to sit by his friend Jenny. I sit alone, holding my backpack to my chest, watching the bus doors close. They're so loud. Everything is. The kids singing and laughing. The music playing from someone's phone nearby.

The seat squeaks as I shuffle my legs. Maybe I was wrong and I'm not ready. I need to be out of that house, though. I've been cooped up inside for too long. I can go outside whenever I want now, and I can talk to anyone, but it all still feels like something I'm not supposed to do. My heart races every time I open my mouth, and I wish I could get my dad's repercussions out of my head, wipe my brain clean of him and all I knew for the first eleven years of my life. He went to prison and is serving time for his crimes. He won't hurt me anymore, and I can finally be who I want to be . . . do what other teenagers do. Sleep in. Watch too much TV. Hang out with friends. Sneak out to parties and go on dates.

Except I don't know how to do any of it without feeling like I need to be punished afterwards. I also know nothing about being someone my age, carefully watching everyone at school and home so I can mimic them the best I can.

When the bus stops in front of our school, I get off after everyone else and head straight inside, the hot sun leaving a warm spot on the back of my neck. I find my locker, place my backpack inside, and take what I need for my first class. I pretend this is a usual day for me. To sit around other people my age and lend someone a pencil when they ask. Taking notes in chemistry and buying pizza from the cafeteria for lunch with money I got from a weekly allowance. I'd hate to get used to it only to have it taken away again.

My stomach twists. I don't want to go back to the group home and wonder if I'll ever see my mom again. I don't want to go back to dad's house either, or the basement storm room. I can be like Nate, can't I? I can be the son my mom always wanted, one she'd never consider leaving behind or sending away. I take a deep breath and keep walking through the crowded hall.

The rest of my day consists of smiling at people in the hallway and making small talk. When I turn toward the guy using the locker next to me, I say hi, and he's friendly back until some football player comes up behind him to whisper something in his ear.

"Oh, shit. You're that freak who should've been locked up with his old man. Yeah, I'll have to talk to someone about getting a new locker. I sure as hell won't be using this one anymore."

"Yeah. You don't want to end up in this guy's basement," his friend jokes, shooting me a glare, and they walk off in the opposite direction together. My chest tightens when I realize how many people heard them. They're all looking at me. The room's closing in on me, the air surrounding me and feeling tight on my skin. It's like I'm being trapped between two heavy walls. My books slip from my hands and I run toward the front exit, slamming into Nate who at first blended in with everyone else.

"Jace," he says almost a little too quietly. "Is everything okay?"

I shake my head, looking back at a group of kids pointing our way with their faces twisted in disgust. "I need to go home."

He nods and takes my hand. "Okay. We can walk there together." There's warmth in his voice and it's almost as comforting as his fingers tangling with mine.

"Yeah. Okay."

"Yeah, go home, freak," someone screams.

"Shh. It's okay. Don't listen to them. They don't know what they're talking about," Nate whispers to me as he tugs me toward the double doors. Some guy blocks our way, grinning. "What do we have here? Freak boyfriends?"

"Fuck off, Kyle," Nate spits. "This is my stepbrother and he's been through a lot, so just get out of our way."

Kyle's jaw tightens and he shoves hard against Nate's chest, nearly knocking him off his feet. "Not until he knows what it's like to be tied up and left in the dark like he did his victims." He grabs me by the collar of my shirt, and Nate tries to stop him from dragging me toward my locker but a group of others hold him back. Kyle removes his belt, and everything happens so fast as he binds my arms behind my back and shoves me inside the cramped space of my locker. I'm scrawny enough to mostly fit, due to my bad eating habits, and whatever part of me doesn't fit gets slammed by the locker door.

My screams cut through the air, and I can hear someone shouting for everyone to get to class. "What's going on out here? Do you have someone in that locker?"

I curl into myself, closing my eyes, when light invades the darkness I was worried would swallow me whole. What they don't realize is that I do know what it's like to be tied and kept in dark places. I was the reason my dad was able to get it right the first time he tricked some young guy into coming home with him from the club.

A hand lands on my shoulder and I shake my head. "I'm sorry," I shout. "I'll do better next time."

"It's okay, sweetheart. It's just me." I open my eyes and the vice principal who I've only met once smiles down at me, her eyes heavy with sympathy. "Those guys will be dealt with accordingly, I promise. Your brother is here and your mom's on her way. Do you think you could take my hand so I can help you out of there?"

I struggle against the belt until I'm able to pull my hands free, my wrists burning from the leather rubbing my skin raw. Sniffling softly, I take her hand and allow her to help me to my feet. Nate rushes my way, pulling me into a hug. I haven't felt one of these since my mom first brought me home. I forgot how nice they were. Why isn't he running away like the others? Why is he still here? I wouldn't have blamed him if he joined them. After all, I deserve it, don't I?

"How about you two come and wait in the office?"

Nate nods against me and pulls away. "Want to come sit with me for a bit?" He grabs my hand, his expression soft.

"Yeah," I say, and I follow him to the principal's office. We sit beside one another in matching purple chairs. The principal asks me if I need anything or if I'm hurt anywhere, and I assure her I'm fine at least three times before she finally gives us some space.

"You didn't run." I tug at the ends of my shirt sleeves, looking everywhere but at him.

"Did you want me to?"

I bite on the inside of my cheek, considering my answer before speaking it out loud. "No. But everyone is usually scared of me. Aren't you?" I finally look at him and his blue eyes hold me hostage. Big and beautiful like the ocean I've only ever seen in movies, giving me a temporary vacation from reality.

He blinks a few times and my palms sweat as he opens his mouth to speak again. "I wasn't sure what to think at first. So many people said you'd end up being like your father. Some of my family call you evil and dangerous. Our parents even worry how everything you went through will affect you later. My mom tried to convince my dad to let me live with her. She said you weren't safe." He takes a breath. "Today, when I searched for the danger and evil they all mentioned, I didn't see it in you. I saw it in everyone else. The way they cornered you like prey, held you down and hurt you. It's why I didn't run—the reason I won't run. I don't think you're like your dad, and you should have at least one person on your side to remind you that you aren't." He smiles softly and my lips copy his.

We don't say anything the rest of the time, and for once silence doesn't feel like a bad thing. Not with Nate next to me, sitting so close to remind me of everything he said he would. Because my dad had proven to be nothing but a monster, and who wants to keep a monster company.

Two

JACE

I skip my locker and go right to class this morning, and I don't pay attention to the faces made behind my back or the paper being tossed at my head before class starts. Nate hangs with his friends most of the day. We don't have any classes together, only lunch. Clutching my lunch bag to my side, I walk to the courtyard and lower myself onto the sidewalk in a hidden spot along the building. The sun feels amazing on my face and I smile up at the birds flying above me.

I really missed a lot before—only being allowed outside when my dad was home, and even then it was limited. I mostly had to stay in the back yard where there weren't any trees or flowers and almost everything growing from the ground was dead. It was a small gated area with a tall wooden fence that made me feel more caged in than the house.

People pass by, not paying me any mind as I scoot closer to the wall, facing away from them. Only three things are in my lunch box, since I said no to almost everything my mom tried to give me. She's been frustrated with how my first week is going, and so am I, but I didn't choose things to go this way. If I could make life easier for her, Terry, and Nate, I would.

Often I worry that all I do is get in the way of their happy little unit. They don't post smiling family pics online anymore. Will I ever know what it's like to be a part of one? I guess we'd all have to be happy in order for the pictures to be good enough to post. Sighing, I stab my Yoo-hoo box with the straw and lean back against the wall, studying the clouds as they form different shapes in the sky.

"That one kind of looks like an alligator eating a donut, don't you think?" Nate sits beside me, setting his food in front of himself. He has a sandwich, grapes, Doritos, and a Sprite. It looks like real food compared to my peanut butter crackers and fruit leather.

"I don't know, I see more of a dinosaur kicking a ball myself," I respond before taking a sip of my drink.

He laughs and his big smile brightens his whole face. Why do I enjoy looking at him so much? Maybe because he's like sunshine after a rainstorm.

"Is that all you're going to eat today?" He points to my sorry excuse for a lunch. It was more than I usually got from my dad, and we'd also had to earn the good snacks at the group home by making progress. That kind of reminded me of my old life. My dad had made me earn things too. A shiver runs through me, and goosebumps cover my skin as I remember the last time I told him I needed new shoes.

"What have you done to earn it?" The memory of his voice is like nails on a chalkboard in my head.

I shrug. "Yeah, I'm not too hungry at school."

"Or at home either." He lifts his sandwich and takes a small bite, mustard dripping over his bottom lip when he sets it down. "Want a bite?"

"No, I'm okay, thanks." I look down at the lettuce hanging out of it, my stomach rumbling. Maybe I do want something more than snacks today. "What is it? Ham and cheese?"

"Nope. Turkey."

My stomach twists and I stiffen.

"What? Did I say something wrong?"

"I don't . . . I'm not a turkey fan." In fact, smelling it now is enough to cause bile to rise in my throat. It's what I used to feed *them*. What he made me give them. Turkey and cheese on white bread with a side of fruit punch.

"No? Is it the taste?" he asks, scooting closer.

"Not exactly. I just don't like it. Can you not get so close with it please."

His forehead wrinkles and he looks down at the sandwich before his eyes meet mine again. "I'm sorry." Panic rises in his voice and he quickly gets to his feet to toss his food away in the nearest trash can.

"What did you do that for?" I ask when he sits back down beside me.

"Seeing you so upset didn't make eating it worth it. I still have my other stuff. I'm not that hungry either." He forces a smile. "Can you tell me what else you don't like so I can be more careful next time?"

I frown. "I'd hate for you to have to give stuff up just for me."

"It's what brothers do, right?" He pops a grape in his mouth, chewing and smiling at the same time. I don't have the heart to tell him he has mustard on his lip, but also don't want him to go the rest of the day walking around with it there, so I grab a napkin from my bag and quickly wipe it away.

"Sorry. It seemed easier in the moment to do it myself instead of telling you. Bad habit." I'm so used to eating with others who can't do things on their own, and I don't know why I can't permanently leave that damn basement.

"It's okay." He takes the napkin from my hand and glances down at the mustard stain. "Thanks. Feel free to stop me from embarrassing myself at school any time you want."

We both laugh and he offers me a grape. I take it, holding the piece of fruit in my hand for a while before finally eating it. I listen to him rant about the songs he has to sing for choir and the guy who always copies him in algebra. I learn more about the things he doesn't like instead of telling him about mine. It buys me a little time until the warning bell rings and we're throwing away all our trash.

"You still haven't told me about what else you don't like."

I zip up my lunch bag and clutch it to my chest. "There are a few random things. Sometimes I don't even remember I hate them until they're brought up."

He nods in understanding and starts walking toward his next class. Mine happens to be close by so I head in the same direction. "How about you tell me as you think of them then?"

"Okay."

Nate says hi to a friend on our way up the stairs, and after he gets his books from his locker some asshole slaps them out of his hand. "Oh, look who it is. The guy who defends kidnapping freaks."

"I don't have time for your shit right now, Kyle. I have to get to class. We all do."

"No one wants you here anymore. I think the both of you should do the whole school a favor and leave."

"Fuck you," Nate blurts, and when he reaches to pick up his books, Kyle shoves him hard to the ground. Anger boils inside me and I quickly move forward, swinging the large book in my hand in the air. The heavy weight comes into contact with his face, knocking the wind out of him. He tumbles to the floor, swearing and gripping his head.

Ignoring the stares, I pick Nate up from the floor, worried I'll find fear in his eyes. But I don't. He wraps his fingers tightly around mine and his blue eyes sparkle with . . . I don't know . . . pride? Triumph? Gratefulness?

I pick up his books and hand them to him right before Kyle lunges at me, tackling me to the ground. We roll around a few times and I manage to dodge his fist more than once. I grab onto his wrist when he swings at me again, twisting hard, and he yelps. It doesn't get him off me, though. With a beet-red face, he's madder than ever, and as he's wrapping his fingers around my neck, someone comes up from behind him, yanking him off.

"Alright everyone, fight's over. Get to class," a man says. I don't recognize him, but judging by his faculty badge he's a teacher. He turns his attention back to us. "You two to the principal's office, now."

"But Jace didn't do anything wrong. He was only defending himself."

"Bullshit. He's a psychopath who probably broke my nose," Kyle protests.

"You're a damn bully," Nate says pointedly. "The only one who should be punished is you."

"Let me handle this, and you get to class like the others," Mr. Smith says sternly.

"But—"

"Either do as I ask or you'll be coming to the principal's office too." Nate shoots me an apologetic look and I smile to let him know it's okay. Seems to be what people do when they want to make another person feel better. It didn't work on me until him.

"Go." Mr. Smith rests his hands on his hips, his expression hard.

Without another word, Nate heads to class, unable to stop looking back at me until he disappears down the hall.

"Come on you two." Mr. Smith waits for us to start walking before he trails behind us. We pick up our pace down the stairs, but my steps slow the closer we get to the front office. Mr. Smith opens the door and only has to give us a look to get us moving again. He tells us to take a seat while he speaks to the principal, and Mrs. Keeley emerges minutes later looking disappointed. "You two again. What happened this time?"

"This freak threatened to kill me and my friends during lunch hour," Kyle lies.

"I never even saw you during lunch hour," I shoot back. "I was eating with Nate in the courtyard and didn't see Kyle until we were on our way to class. He attacked us first."

"Is this true, Mr. Johnson?"

"No," he says firmly with a gleam in his eye. I really don't like this guy.

"*Sometimes you have to fight to remain the one in control. If you don't take them down, they'll take you down.*"

I resist the urge to pound my dad's word from my head. They come to me every time I'm scared. I used to cling to them as a lifeline, and I feel like I still do in unexpected situations. They happen so fast and I react on instinct—the one thing I've used to protect myself this whole time.

"He's lying," I say. "He approached us in the hall, telling us we should do the school a favor and leave, then shoved Nate when we tried to ignore him."

"Come on, Mrs. Keeley. You can't possibly believe this criminal over me. Look what he did to my nose."

She sighs, pinching between her brows. "I'll be calling both your parents today, and I want you both to attend detention for the week."

"What?" Kyle's muscles bulge in his face. "You can't be serious."

"Yes, and if you keep lashing out, Mr. Johnson, I'll make it two weeks. Head to the nurse's office and have her look at your nose. Maybe she can get you some ice too. And Mr. Thompson." her heavy gaze lands on me. "Go on and head to class."

Kyle huffs in annoyance and I quietly grab my backpack, doing as she asks. The rest of the day drags out, especially when I finally reach detention.

At least being quiet and listening to instructions has never been a problem for me. Kyle keeps trying to pull his phone out when he thinks no one's looking, eventually getting it taken away. His nose didn't end up being broken, only bruised, and while he holds a bag of ice to his face, I focus on the paper they're making us write. I don't put my pencil down until it's time to leave. Kyle, being the asshole he is, slams his shoulder into mine as soon as we're outside the classroom, flipping me the bird. "You better watch yourself, freak."

Clenching my fists at my side, I inhale deeply and then exhale, reminding myself he isn't worth it, and my anger diminishes when Nate comes around the corner, rushing my way. He takes me in his arms. "I'm so glad you're okay," he says. "Want to take the bus home with me? I think it's better not to deal with Mom and Dad until we have to. The next one will be here in fifteen minutes." He steps back a little, his blue eyes catching the light from a nearby window and I no longer have to remind myself of anything.

"Yeah. Let's go home." Maybe if I say it enough, it'll eventually feel that way. When Nate takes my hand and guides me outside, I'm given hope that anything is possible.

Three

JACE

Sixteen years old

Today is my birthday and Nate's made sure to remind me all week. Mom gave me the option of either a party or fancy dinner. I chose dinner. In order to have a party, you need friends to invite, and the only one I have is my brother. The title's become easier to use the more we've spent time together. I've defended him at school and he's defended me at home, constantly coming to my rescue. Nate's made it easier to be here. Easier to breathe. I'm never too quiet for him, too awkward or weird. He doesn't see me for all the mistakes I've made.

Last year, when Nate handed me a cupcake, I crushed it between my fingers without thinking, going from smiling to fuming with anger in an instant. Instead of getting mad, he rested a hand on my shoulder and said, *"You don't like cupcakes for your birthday."* It was a statement, not a question. He automatically added to my "don't like" list whenever I reacted badly to something, and waited until I was ready to tell him why instead of forcing the answers out of me like everyone else. Unlike my mom, Nate took the time to understand me and help me understand myself.

"I think you're going to love this gift better than last year's," Nate says, interrupting my thoughts as he makes himself comfortable on my bed. Leaning against my dresser, I smirk his way. "Oh yeah?"

"Yup. But I've decided to give it to you later instead of at dinner."

Growing more curious, I approach the bed. "Is it something embarrassing?"

He shakes his head, his brown curls bouncing. "Nope. Just something I don't think anyone would understand but me and you."

"Hmm. Well now I want to open it before dinner." I sit down beside him and he bumps me with his leg. Small rips cover his dark jeans, and as he lifts himself higher on his elbows, his stomach becomes fully exposed below his pink crop top. He's been wearing them a lot more lately. His style has drastically changed over the last year and I find it more fitting. His dad, on the other hand, keeps hoping it'll be a phase that ends soon.

"Too bad." He sticks out his pink tongue. "You'll have to be patient."

I thought I was good at waiting until Nate made me eager for everything—to see my first movie in theaters, play at the arcade, go on rides at the carnival, and for something as simple as a birthday gift.

"Fine," I breathe out, shooting him a glare. "We're still going to ride the Ferris wheel later, right?"

"Yup." His face lights up. Whenever I wake up from a bad nightmare, I think of moments like this, replacing the angry and scared faces with his. If only I could stop seeing them. They continue to haunt me and I worry they always will. Especially the last man my dad took. His tears, bloody face, and convulsing body are still fresh in my mind, almost as if they happened yesterday.

"Need a major distraction?" he asks, almost as if he can read my mind.

I nod. "Always." He bounces on the bed and grabs the pillow.

"What are you doing?"

"Giving you what you need with a pillow fight." He whacks me on the shoulder, laughing.

My heart warms at the wonderful sound and I grab another pillow. We knock each other around the bed, laughing, and end up on the floor with me on top of his smaller body.

"Get off me. I can't breathe." He laughs harder and I tickle his sides before rolling onto the space beside him.

"Who'll be at the dinner?" I ask, trying to catch my breath.

"Mom, Dad, me, you, and the grandparents. Oh, and Aunt Tracy. Not sure whether she's bringing her killjoy of a husband, but Rachel and Andy are most likely coming. Hopefully they'll actually sit down and eat this time instead of playing tag around the restaurant."

I blow out a longer breath. "Will you sit next to me?" I turn my face toward him.

He smiles and grabs my hand. "Duh. If you don't want to go, we can always make something up. Say you're sick."

I shake my head, looking back at the ceiling. "No. I'll go. What could be so bad about having dinner with my family on my birthday? Besides, I'm mostly going for the lobster."

"Me too, and I guess I can also help you celebrate turning sixteen while I'm there." He grins from ear to ear.

We're all at the restaurant enjoying dinner in between small talk until our evening goes from decent to bad in a matter of minutes. One of my little cousins chooses to sit beside me and show me his game. We're having fun, collecting mushrooms, until my aunt yanks him away from me, pointing a finger in my face to stay away from her son. She was so focused on her wine and arguing with her husband that it took her a while to notice her son had switched seats.

"Go sit with your dad, sweetie." She shoves my cousin to the other end of the table before looking back at me with her whole face tensing. "You stay away from my son. Who's to say you can be trusted around children. Don't think I haven't heard about you trying to drug Nate."

"Tracy, not here," my mom warns.

"I think you need to leave before things get further out of hand than they already have," Terry says and he gets up to whisper in Nate's ear, sliding something into his hand before signaling to our waiter.

My mom and Tracy end up in a full-blown argument and people from nearby tables start staring our way. I bury my face in my hands, wishing the floor would swallow me whole, and then a hand squeezes my arm. "I think there's a roller coaster calling your name not far from here. How about we answer it?"

I open my eyes and Nate pulls my face toward his so I don't see anything else but him. "What do you say?"

"Just the two of us?"

He smiles softly. "Just the two of us."

We rise from our chairs and I don't look at anything but him as we make our way out of the restaurant. My mom's and aunt's voices disappear behind us the closer we get to the exit. Once outside, I relax a little, breathing in the night's fresh air before following Nate to our parents' car.

"What are we doing?" I ask, my hand freezing on the passenger door handle.

"Getting out of here. Dad gave me his keys and said they'd find another way home." He gets into the car and I follow him, strapping into my seat belt once I'm sitting comfortably beside him.

Nate starts the car and quickly pulls out of the parking lot. I hold on to the side of the door, closing my eyes as he speeds up then swerves a little as he takes the first turn. He got his license recently, and riding with him makes me nervous because he's got a lot more learning to do. At least he's driving; I'm still trying to get used to riding in cars. My stomach hasn't stopped feeling uneasy since the first time, because when I said I never left the house with my dad, I meant it. I took the bus to school the one year I went, but it was so long ago it remains a blur. The bus doesn't bother me, though. My dad didn't make deliveries by bus. My breaths quicken and I squeeze my legs together.

"Am I going too fast?"

I don't say anything and look down at the floorboard. He squeezes my hand. "I'm sorry, brother. I'll slow down."

He gives me a sense of importance when he calls me that. For a little while, I feel like I belong. The car slows and my shoulders drop, my stomach settling a little when I see lit-up rides ahead. "We're getting close."

"Yeah," he agrees, pulling into the cramped parking lot.

There are a lot of people here. My throat goes dry when the car stops. "It's a bit crowded."

"Don't worry about them. We're here for you, remember?"

"Yeah." I wait for him to walk over to open my door before getting out.

"Shall we go straight to the Ferris wheel?"

"Sure," I say, glancing around, feeling a little overwhelmed.

"Or we can go back to the car." He loops his arm in mine, leaning into my body.

I shake my head. "I'd rather be here than at home. My mind is spinning out of control and I need to keep busy or else it'll take over."

"Then let's find something that'll make you focus on the world spinning instead." He drags me to the ticket booth and purchases two bracelets.

Laughter and excited screams surround us as he drags me to a short line of people. They all enter a gate leading to purple pod-looking things.

"What is this?"

"You'll see." We walk forward and he grabs my hand to hold up my wrist. A man who was collecting tickets before nods at us and gestures for us to keep moving. We stop when we finally come across an empty ride. I slide in first and Nate squeezes in beside me, placing his hands on a black wheel in the center. I put my hands next to his and he crosses our arms bumping shoulders with me. "When the ride starts, we have to spin the wheel as hard and fast as we can."

We move slowly at first and speed up as we loop around. Going faster and faster, we crash against each other, struggling to sit up straight. Metal scraping metal mixes with loud wind and our laughter. Our hands occasionally land on each other as we spin the wheel. He's right. I'm too focused on my racing heart and jump in my stomach to think about anything else. His face lands in my neck and he leaves it there, his hands staying on mine until the ride ends.

"Sorry, got a little dizzy and you make a good headrest."

"Can we go again?" I ask, staying exactly where I am while everyone else exits the ride.

"We can go as many times as you want."

My stomach flutters, and I don't understand what this feeling is but I'm not ready to walk away from it. I realize it's not the ride taking me away from everything bad that happened today—it's him.

We ride the spinning saucers five more times before finally making our way to the Ferris wheel. Being so high above the ground feels better than I thought it would. I'm far away from other people's judgment and don't have to worry whether anyone will recognize me. I'm far away from my aunt and the restaurant. Far away from my dad and our basement. It's only me and Nate.

I don't enjoy the carousel as much as the flying swings. I also worry I'm consuming way too much sugar between all the rides with the copious amounts of stuffed Oreos, cotton candy, and funnel cake I consume.

"I think my stomach is going to combust if I eat any more."

Nate laughs, squeezing his new pink bear that I won him. He looks so small holding it, with it being half his size. A quick breeze blows his hair away from his face and I notice the light pink scar there for the very first time. He could have a million of them on his face and still be beautiful.

"What happened there?" I sweep my fingers over the scar.

"Fell off my cousin's bunk beds when I was six. Hit the bottom bed frame pretty hard and had to get stitches."

Him telling me something about himself makes me want to suddenly give him something in return. "I hate chamomile tea." My dad made it for every guy he brought home when they wouldn't stop making too much noise. I had to carry it down to the basement, the leafy scent wafting into my nose.

His eyes widen. He usually has to learn what I don't like through experimentation and not from my own words. He smiles and playfully bumps my shoulder. "Then I'll remember to get rid of every bag mom has in the kitchen when we get home."

We walk around a little longer and people-watch before heading back to the house. The car is filled with old Britney Spears songs and Nate's off-pitch singing the whole ride there. He never lets the car go silent for long and sings even louder when we're walking to the front door, his voice going quiet when we walk inside.

My mom is standing behind the center island in the kitchen with a birthday cake resting in front of her. "Happy Birthday, Jace," is written in blue words on top of white icing.

"I'm glad you boys made it home safely. Have a good time?" Her red-rimmed eyes are hard to miss when Nate flips the main kitchen light on. Now I know why she was standing in the dark with only the stove light on.

"Yeah. I ate way too much, though." I rub my stomach and she smiles.

"What are you doing in here alone?" Nate asks, inching closer to the cake.

"I didn't want to miss y'all coming in. We didn't get a chance to sing you happy birthday. I've already missed so many birthdays . . ." Her words trail off and her eyes water. "I don't want to miss any more."

My throat clogs with emotion and I stand beside her, holding her hand. "It's a really great cake, Mom," I say, feeling like I'm still trying the name out for size and it doesn't exactly fit yet.

"It really is," Nate agrees. "Let me grab the candles."

We light the candles, and they both sing happy birthday. Smoke rises in the air as I blow them out without making a wish. I never believed in that sort of thing. It never helped me before—not wishes or prayers. No matter how much I shouted at the sky, no one ever heard me or came to my rescue. No one made Dad's anger settle or his hands feel any lighter when he used them against me. In the end I helped myself without realizing what I was doing.

No matter how full Nate and I are, we take a slice of cake from my mom, and it's not until our plates are empty that she hugs us both goodnight. While she's handling the mess, Nate drags me to his room and pulls out something wrapped in snowman wrapping paper. "I forgot to grab a birthday bag from the store and didn't have time to get one today."

I take it from his hand and we both sit on the bed. The paper rips beneath my hands and I can't help but smile big when I see what's underneath. A blue notebook that says *All the Things That Make Jace a Good Person* on the front.

We open it together and he points to the first one. "He always holds the door open for others."

"That's not a big deal," I huff out.

He turns the page and says, "Shares his candy with me."

"I can't eat all that sugar alone," I smirk.

The next page says, "Always lets me have the last soda and ice cream."

They're all little acts of kindness, but Nate makes a big deal out of each one, and all I see right now is what he sees—he's happy with me exactly the way I am. Who cares if the rest of the world keeps their distance from me when Nate never lets anyone stop him from running toward me.

Four

JACE

Eighteen years old

"You look so handsome," my mom says, straightening Nate's pink jacket. Glitter shines along the lapels, matching his eyeshadow.

"When's Rick supposed to come?" I ask, plopping down on the couch with a water bottle clutched between my fingers.

He sighs, running a hand through his perfect, thick dark locks. "Any minute now hopefully." Nate's gaze drifts to me. "You sure I can't talk you into being our third wheel tonight?"

I cringe. "I'm sure. Rick hates me anyway and would probably just call me a cock block like the last time I tagged along with y'all to the movies."

"Language," my mom warns.

Nate and I laugh as he lowers himself beside me on the couch. An engine roars outside and he perks up, looking out the window behind us. Hope diminishes in his eyes when his dad walks through the door, and Nate looks down at his phone. As he starts to look away, it buzzes in his hands, and the light in his eyes leaves as fast as it comes.

"What is it?" I ask, scooting closer.

His shoulders droop and his eyes water. "Rick's not coming."

"What do you mean he's not coming?" I ask, my stomach sinking at the sense of loss in his eyes. My parents are in the kitchen, chatting about some office party at my stepdad's work, not paying us any attention. Good. If they were, Nate would probably pretend everything was okay and shrug it all off.

"He said he has to help his dad with something." He huffs out a breath, his frown breaking my heart. "I don't understand. We've been planning this for months. We even picked out outfits together to make sure we matched." His eyes are sunken in when he looks at me and I sigh, resting a hand on his leg.

"I guess going to prom wouldn't be the worst thing I could do tonight. Got a tux I can borrow?"

His eyes light up and he throws his arms around me, embracing me in a suffocating hug. I'm already missing his warmth when he pulls away full of smiles. My heart skips a beat when he wraps his fingers around mine and drags me to his room. I don't know why, but that's been happening more and more lately—the weird flutters in my chest and stomach. They don't typically come this easily, but lately all it takes is for him to look my way for me to feel like my feet are lifting off the ground. I wasn't aware of what I'd do for that smile until he needed me, like now.

Fuck that asshole who stood him up. He's an idiot and doesn't deserve Nate's time. Maybe I don't either but I won't say no when he offers to give it to me. He leads me to his closet, tossing an array of clothes on the bed. Minutes later, I settle on a pair of black slacks and a black button-down, the material around my arms a little snug. We're basically the same size, except I'm bulky in some areas he isn't. Hating how helpless and weak I'd been against my dad, I started doing push-ups and lifting weights before eventually joining the wrestling team.

I didn't want to be the defenseless, scrawny kid who fit perfectly inside small places anymore, and maybe that's also part of the reason I can't seem to stay out of school fights. The spiteful words and name-calling toward me I could handle. It was when they aimed them all at Nate that caused anger to boil inside me. My blood felt hot in my veins whenever he was threatened in any way. He's my brother, my best friend, the only reason for me to smile and laugh anymore.

I finish getting ready, unable to avoid Nate's gelled fingers sweeping through my hair. He fixes my folded collar and undoes the top button, his fingers burning a hole through my skin everywhere they touch. I didn't think much of how he made me feel until recently, but with us being older and him dating people it's getting harder to ignore. I don't like Rick or any guy who flirts or touches him too much.

"Ready?" He runs his fingers through my hair one more time, his face beaming the way I love.

"Yeah. Let's go drink spiked punch and dance the night away to horrible music."

Laughing, he shakes his head. "As if I'll ever be able to convince you to come out onto the dance floor."

It's crazy to me that after all this time he doesn't realize I'd move the fucking earth for him if he asked. Maybe because he's never pushed me into doing anything, I just always volunteer. He doesn't like me to feel pressured or to go out of my comfort zone in order to make someone else happy. It's hard to even notice anymore when I naturally gravitate in his direction. I hated the idea of him going to prom with that asshole, and kept picturing myself squeezing beside him in the limo, holding his hand. It's not that I didn't want to do these things before, I just didn't realize I did until he was doing them with me. Us alone. Not me as some third wheeler.

We're unable to stop my mom gushing over us and being blinded by her camera's flash a gazillion times before finally making it out the door. A white limo awaits us out front and the driver opens the back door so we can slide in one by one. Our parents wave at us from the porch, shouting at us to have a good time, more pictures being snapped until we're no longer in their view.

Nate opens the rooftop window and briefly sticks his head out before being yelled at by the driver to sit back down in his seat. We giggle as he crashes back beside me, nearly landing in my lap. "I've always wanted to do that," he quips.

When we finally arrive at the school, Nate snaps a picture of us in the limo before sliding out first. Following behind him, I take in all the girls in pretty dresses and guys wearing tuxes, some too big to fit their bodies properly, clearly rented.

Nate grabs my hand, dragging me inside between moving bodies and we hand a girl at a table our tickets—his and Rick's tickets. As much as I hate Nate being stood up, I'm happy to be the one to share such a special night with him. This doesn't mean as much to me as it does to him, though. None of it did. Not senior skip day, getting my yearbook signed, going to all the last school parties, or graduating. I know I should be grateful for the opportunity to enjoy all these things, but I still don't feel like it's my life I'm living half the time.

All of this is the normal routine of a teenager, but I can't stop seeing myself ending up in a basement at the end of the night. I hate dark places, even when lit up with fairy lights, but as long as my eyes remain on Nate, I'm able to pretend every place we walk into is as bright as a hot summer's day.

"You okay?" he asks, as we stand in line to have one of those scrapbook moments captured by some professional photographer the school hired.

"Yeah," I reassure him, moving with the people in front of us. "You enjoying yourself so far?"

"I think so. Then again we only got here ten minutes ago and I haven't had to talk to anyone I try to avoid at school yet."

Snorting, I shove him forward when it's our turn to get our picture taken. Picking up a few things from one of the tables nearby, he hands me large glasses and a funny hat. He's wearing a pink boa and golden crown, smiling widely beside me and holding bunny ears behind my head. Not your typical couple photo but it's us in a nutshell. With Nate, it's easy to pretend life has always been this way.

We spend the next few hours laughing with friends, dancing the electric slide under strobe lights, and stuffing our faces with too many snacks, then right when I think our night is coming to an end, we're invited to an after-prom party. The limo driver drops us off in front of the school quarterback's house. So many cars already cram the streets.

Nate is chatting with different people on our way inside and then freezes as soon as he enters the living room. In front of a keg unfolds a scene neither of us was expecting. The night started out shaky but I thought we would both remain on steady ground at least until morning came.

I couldn't have been more wrong. Rick's kissing someone else. A girl has her arms around his neck, shoving her tongue into his willingly open mouth. He doesn't see us at first. Nate is shell-shocked, his mouth agape and eyes wide. I've never wanted to hurt anyone more. Before I can drag Nate out of the house, Rick looks right at us, his eyes wild and face flushed. "Nate. I didn't think you'd be here."

"And I thought you were supposed to be helping your dad."

"I was . . ."

"But then decided to come to a party afterward and suck face with some cheerleader instead of asking your boyfriend to meet up."

Rick rubs a hand over his face, looking more pleased with himself than sorry. I swear if we stay here any longer, I won't be able to resist punching the jerk's lights out.

"I really don't know what to say other than I'm tired of waiting around for you. Let's be real. This wasn't ever going to go past a few closed-mouth kisses in front of your locker, and a guy like me has needs, baby."

"I'm not your baby," Nate spits out. "And stay the hell away from me."

Nate rushes out the front door, and when Rick tries to follow him, I slam my hand hard against his chest. "Don't even fucking think about it."

"What are you, like his savior or something? How is any guy supposed to get past first base with you always hovering? Maybe it's time you learn to be obsessed with someone else besides your own brother."

My blood runs cold, and tired of seeing the grin on his face, I quickly lift my hand and my fist meets with his nose. My ears are met with a cracking sound and I reach back and slam into him again, hitting his cheek this time, knocking his ass to the ground.

Spitting out blood, Rick grabs his nose. "What the fuck, freak."

"Hey, no fucking fights in the house. Take that shit outside." Garrett's gaze turns to ice when his eyes finally meet mine. "Who the fuck invited you anyway? Guys like you don't belong in places like this."

"Guys like him don't belong anywhere but a fucking jail cell," someone shouts from the large, gathering crowd.

"Don't worry. I don't want to be here anyway." Rushing away, I don't look back until my face is hit by a slight breeze and the smell of wet grass. They're all staring at me, their faces threatening like some fucking angry mob.

"What are you waiting for? Get the fuck off my lawn, freak show."

My whole body vibrates with anger, and I don't calm down until I spot Nate sitting on a bench alone across the way at some park. I choose him. I'll always choose him. Flipping Garrett off, I go in the one direction my heart never has trouble following. As I'm sitting down, I say the first thing on my mind. "I'm sorry about Rick."

Lowering his head, he digs his fingers into his knees. "Yeah. It was only a matter of time before something like that happened with a guy like him."

"Doesn't make it any better."

He shrugs, sighing. "I guess I keep trying to see the good in everyone but it doesn't always turn out the way it has with you."

He says that because he doesn't know the inner thoughts I struggle with daily. He can't see my dreams, and I don't act on many of the instinctual urges that were built into me a long time ago.

"You can't talk to people on the outside. They're dangerous. They'll undo all the good we've done. They'll get in the way of our calling to help others."

Squeezing my eyes shut, I take a breath. It wasn't good, what we did. It was evil. I wish I could stop questioning myself on whether I was wrong to run away. Whether I was wrong to reveal my dad for the monster he was. It had to be done and I know it did. This is the life I need to connect with, but how can I when half of me can't leave that fucking basement or be rid of the mindset that Nate should be tied up when I talk to him, for both of our safety.

"I wish I could see only what you see when you look at me."

"I wish you could too." He lifts my hand and places a lightning bug on my palm. Glowing brightly, the small creature flaps its wings and I'm mesmerized by its ability to be brave enough to stay where it is.

"I think it can see it too. It stays because it feels safe. The same reason I do." Linking his arm in mine, he rests his head on my shoulder and watches the lightning bug circle us a few times before flying away. The sky is dark but all I can focus on is the bug's light, and when it's fully gone Nate takes its place, and for a little while I forget about the dark basement and my life before. I forget about my worries of becoming the man my father would be proud of—the one I turn into in my nightmares.

Five

JACE

Nineteen years old

"We did it! We survived high school." Nate wraps his arms around me, kissing me on the cheek. Not sure what made him start doing that but I remember when it first happened. Six months ago, when he'd wished me a happy birthday, he pressed his warm, soft lips to my cheek and I immediately became addicted.

"We did," I agree. Shouldn't I feel more joy over graduating? It's a big deal, isn't it? To get honors and be accepted into a four-year college of my choice.

It had been like the separation was happening all over again while I waited for my name to be called earlier. I was standing on the ceiling, watching my life unfold from someone else's viewpoint as whispers filled my ears.

"He shouldn't even be allowed on stage with the other kids," one woman said.

"Probably the only time he'll make his mother proud," another spoke in a hushed whisper. *Not low enough for me not to hear. Your ears grow more sensitive when you spend so much time in the dark. "I know guys like him. He'll get bored and hurt someone. Guys corrupted from a young age usually do,"* she continued.

More words had wrapped around me until my head spun and Nate took my hand, helping me leave them all behind before accepting my diploma. Yeah, we really did do it. Together. He made it easier to walk a straight line—to head in the right direction—because it always led to him. Getting great grades in school will get us into the same college, and graduating together will let us leave for college at the same time and avoid the bullies who kept me by his side at school when he needed me most.

"I'm so proud of my boys," my mom says from beside us, my stepdad smiling as he wraps his arm around her. Or I should say, my official dad on paper. He's been trying to adopt me for a long time and it finally went through last month. My dad fought to keep his rights and my mom fought even harder to have them taken away. She won, but then she also gained a new problem with me being her prize. Why did she want me so badly? Why now? There are still things I don't understand about her leaving me behind with him, and her constantly saying she never wanted to be without me messes with my head too much.

"Know that I always wanted you here. Not a day went by while you were gone that I didn't think about you," she said to me on my eighteenth birthday, only months ago.

Yet she left me to suffer for eleven years. The worst part is, some of the memories of my dad still show up in my head as fond ones. They were our best days together, but my mom has shown me over the years that there was nothing good about them. Doesn't she understand? She's part of the reason my brain is broken. I didn't realize I needed to be saved. I didn't know there was a better life out there. It's hard to when you're taught at a young age to view your monster as a hero.

"How about one more picture before you two leave us for the next three days?" my stepdad says, pulling me from my reverie.

"But my hair's all messed up from my hat," Nate whines in the cute way he sometimes does.

"Then put your hat back on. Problem solved." I ruffle his hair and he elbows me in the side.

"You and your bright ideas."

"That is why they call me the smart brother," I deadpan and Nate shoots me a glare.

"Literally no one has ever called you that."

"Alright, you two goofballs look this way and smile." Terry lifts his phone while Nate is adjusting the hat on his head. He smells like peppermint and honey when he presses his cheek to mine, my arm wrapping around his shoulder as we "cheese" big for our parents.

"This one's definitely going on the main living-room wall," Terry says, showing my mom. She beams, holding a hand to her chest.

"You sure you both wouldn't rather come to dinner with me and Dad instead of meeting your friends to go camping?"

Nate rolls his eyes. "We've had dinner with you guys every day for like the last hundred years."

"I think your brother is definitely right to call himself the smarter one based on your counting skills," Terry jokes.

We all erupt into laughter before hugging our parents goodbye, promising my mom we'll take her to a fancy restaurant and buy her the most expensive meal on the menu when we get back home.

"You both be careful. Call us if you need anything." My mom waves our way and we slip into Nate's car.

"Bye. Stay out of trouble while we're gone," Nate shouts, sliding into the driver side.

"I hope you packed lots of sunscreen," I say, glancing over at Nate's pale skin. The guy turns red after standing in the sun for five minutes, never failing to come home with sunburn after our days spent at the pool during summer.

"And I hope your ass gets in the water with me."

Tugging on my seat belt, I buckle in as he pulls out of the packed parking lot, people rushing between cars to meet up with friends and family.

"I'll think about it."

"You always say that. We've been to the pool together how many times? And you've yet to dip more than a toe in."

I snort, searching through the playlist on his phone. "Then I promise to at least dip a whole foot in this time if it'll make you happy."

"Pretty sure you owe me a whole two legs at this point."

"Sounds like you're placing a KFC order."

Shaking his head, he side-eyes me as I hit play on one of his many summer mixes. "Cool for the Summer" by Demi Lovato plays and he turns up the volume, drowning out my singing.

"On second thought, I think I'll just drown your ass when we get there."

I laugh and he shouts the lyrics at the top of his lungs, not taking more than a few seconds between songs to rest his vocal cords the whole way there. Several of Nate's friends already have their tents set up by the time we park and get out. Hot dogs and hamburgers are on the grill, music playing while two cheerleaders dance on one of the picnic tables.

Inching closer to Nate, I whisper in his ear, "Why did I agree to come again?"

"Because you love me and you've never been to a lake before."

He got me on both counts for sure. I've dreamed about the beaches I've seen on TV so many times, and this is probably as close as I'll ever come to one. I'm still having too much trouble adapting to the world around me to travel anywhere too far from home, and I don't know if I'll ever be ready. Being out here in a new place only an hour away is terrifying enough. "Maybe," I say, smirking.

"I think you'll be much happier once we get our tent set up and we're roasting s'mores on the fire."

I'll be better once it's only us. Sure, I'll get to see a lake in person for the first time, but I'll also be sharing a small tent with Nate, sleeping right next to him. We've fallen asleep on the couch next to each other before but this feels different somehow. I'll get to wake up, turn around, and see his face. How does he sleep when he's under the covers now that he's older? Does he still wear cute pajamas with fireflies on them, or does he wear less clothes?

Heat spreads in my groin, and this has been something that only started happening after I noticed how good his lips felt on my skin. Fuck. He's my stepbrother—well, my adopted brother now—but shit, I'd be lying if I said I hadn't wanted his lips to move a little to the left earlier. It's not like we're blood related, and we didn't exactly grow up together.

"Want to eat before I put you to work?" His words pull me away from my conflicted thoughts.

"Put me to work, huh? This means I'm putting that tent together all by myself, doesn't it?"

He purses his lips, batting his lashes. "You know how uncoordinated I am. I'll just get in the way. You'll be more productive without me."

I roll my eyes. "And what will you be doing? Sitting pretty in a chair, watching me do all the hard work?"

A pretty blush spreads across his cheeks. "I like to call it supervising."

Sputtering a laugh, I shake my head. "Yeah, okay Mr. Supervisor. How about you add a hotdog on top of that." His laughter drifts off into the distance as I head for the car to collect the tent from the trunk. My stomach clenches when I see Rick laughing with another guy from the football team. Of course his ass is here. Maybe they ruled high school, but they won't be shit to anyone in college. Rick didn't get the football scholarship he'd hoped for. I couldn't help but smile at that. It's not often guys like him get what they deserve.

Rick's smile falls when his eyes land on me, and his friend looks my way when he whispers something in his ear. I grab the tent and our bags, looking anywhere other than where the loud snickering is coming from.

"Look. Nate brought his dog with him," Rick's friend chimes.

"Nah, dogs are more civilized than that freak. He better set his tent up far away from everyone else's. Who knows what kind of shit he'll pull when we're all sleeping."

I keep walking, ignoring them like I have been during our last weeks of school. I'm too close to being out of here with Nate to fuck up now. At first I didn't want to go to school in another city, but the thought of being far away from these fuckers and this gossiping town increases the appeal.

"Everything okay?" Nate pulls a bottle of water from an ice chest, water dripping from the plastic.

"Yeah. Just Rick being his usual asshole self."

Anger flashes in Nate's big blue eyes. "What did he say?"

I drop everything to the ground and wave him off. "Nothing. It's not important. Where's this hotdog you were supposed to be getting me?"

His smile is back, and if only it were possible to wrap myself in it and get forever lost in the hope it gives me. "Oh, right." He takes a swig of his water. "I'll be back."

In only ten minutes, I have the tarp for the pop-up tent fully open, and Nate returns carrying plates in both hands and a chair under his arm. Balancing the plates on top of one another in one hand, careful not to drop our food, he unfolds the chair as best he can with the other. Jumping to his rescue, I grab the food from him before it can all crash to the ground. "Looks like I need to supervise you instead."

He swats me away, straightening out his chair before sitting down. "Is that your way of thanking me for getting you food?"

"No. My thanks happened when I stopped you from feeding the ground instead of us." I wink, handing him his plate.

I open a chair next to his and we eat our food in mostly silence, taking in the noises of nature. Chirping, buzzing, and swaying branches. Large trees look like they're touching the sky, and birds fly above the setting sun.

"So this is camping?"

Nate smiles, swallowing his last bite of hotdog. "Yup, and it's only going to get worse from here."

After we have the tent fully set up and where we want it, far from the others, we lay out our sleeping bags next to each other. Nate grabs our bags from the car and I examine our camping area before settling in front of the fire with some of the others. Rick and his girlfriend are out swimming in the lake, and I'm able to relax a lot easier with him gone. Nate's latest crush, Gabe, hands me a beer and smiles down at me. "You need to loosen up a bit man. Have fun. Relax and shoot the shit. This is our last summer of not having to worry about adult responsibilities."

"Right," I respond, twisting the cap open with my palm and pocketing my trash, not wanting to join in on everyone else's littering frenzy. Gabe plops down into one of the chairs next to me, not deliberately avoiding me the way the rest of his friends do, and when Nate's finished laughing with some girl he hardly talked to at school, he turns to me and whispers, "Remind me to add 'cares about the earth too much' to your notebook when we get home."

I stifle a laugh, rolling my eyes, and he leans his shoulder against mine, his eyes glowing from the fire. I'm here for him. I'll go anywhere he asks me even if I don't care for anyone else around us.

"So who's going to tell the first spooky story?" Gabe asks before sipping his beer.

"Oh, I will," one girl says, raising her hand. It's hard to keep up with all these people's names, especially when they all dress and act alike. Why does Nate hang out with these assholes? I guess Gabe isn't so bad, but he also isn't my favorite person either.

Even though Nate never admitted it, I know Gabe is the real reason for him coming. At least the main selling point. I mean, I guess I get it. The guy's charming, classically handsome, with perfect hair. Not to mention his mom isn't married to Nate's dad.

Would it really make a difference anyway? Nate and I probably wouldn't be as close as we are if we didn't live together. He'd still talk to me, though, only because he has a thing for rescuing wounded wild animals who no one else wants to be around. I'm very similar to the malnourished one-eyed kitten he picked up from the road three days ago and took home to nurture back to health.

The only difference is, the kitten has a better chance in blending back in with society than I do. He has a defect on the outside which people will overlook in time, but no one here will ever forget where I came from and what I did before. It's an inner demon they assume I'll always carry, eventually going off like a ticking time bomb.

I know they're all waiting for it with bated breath by the way they keep their distance at the grocery store and leave the church bench my family sits at mostly empty. The kitten will go on to be like the rest of his kind, with his other senses heightening to make up for the lost eye. I, on the other hand, am as unpredictable as the man who raised me, hiding a dark side that has yet to be discovered.

They won't ever stop reminding me I'm the same as my father, and Nate won't stop pointing out all the ways I'm different.

"Your dad is the nightmare people ran from, and you are the type of person who wakes them up so they can be okay again," he told me once, as we sat in an abandoned tree house in the woods behind our house.

Nate perks up beside me, a red solo cup in hand with something amber colored swirling inside as he rests it in the cup holder. "Oh, is it that time already? I love camp stories."

"Yup, and Tina's up first. Let's see what you got. I better be scared shitless soon."

Tina laughs, scooting to the edge of her seat. Clearing her throat, she sits up tall and presses her palms to her knees. "It all started with a man named Cole. He was very plain and ordinary looking. Like every other thirty-something-year-old, he yearned for more than the life he had. The white picket fence, wife, and adorable baby boy no longer satisfied him." She takes a breath before continuing, everyone eyeing her closely with intense gazes, including me. "It started with picking up men at clubs for nothing more than innocent conversation, but quickly turned into dirty hook-ups in bathroom stalls and the back of his blue pickup. His wife learned of his endeavors and threatened to leave, but he wouldn't have that, so he started hitting her, leaving her weak and helpless after every fight."

"This doesn't sound like a ghost story to me," one guy says.

"You guys wanted scary and that's what I'm giving you. Now, can I keep going or not?" She shoots me a smile, a glint in her eyes. Gnawing fills my stomach. I have a really bad feeling about where this is going.

"Yes, please do," Gabe encourages and I scratch at my knees nervously. This story sounds like one I've heard before, and that's because it is. She doesn't have to talk much longer for me to know what direction she's heading in, mentioning men kept in the basement as sex slaves. The moment she brings up the emotionless boy who was too eager to make his dad proud, I shoot up from my chair and head through a grouping of trees. A mixture of laughing and yelling fades in the distance. I don't have to look to know the person jumping to my defense is Nate.

Footsteps trail behind me, leaves crunching loudly the closer they get. "Jace," Nate's whispers mix in with the slight breeze.

"Go back to your friends," I say, pressing my face to the tree bark, suppressing my tears. They won't see me cry. They can never see me cry. No matter what. Crying was also against the rules, and I wait for my father to pop out at any moment to remind me with his closed fists or by dunking my head in the dirty sink water.

"If you want to go home, we can."

Sniffling, I lift my face and shake my head. "No. This is supposed to be the highlight of your whole summer."

A hand rests on my shoulder and his lips press to my ear. "No. Spending this time with you is. Let's get out of here and camp out in the old tree house instead."

Turning around, I swipe hair from his face. "I won't let them chase me away every time. Besides, we don't have to see them after this." I hate the idea of them ruining this for him.

"You sure?"

"Yeah. It's not like I haven't heard it all before."

"You shouldn't have to hear it at all. Ever." Wrapping his arms around me, he buries his face in my neck. Holding him closer to my body, I turn my nose into his hair, inhaling the fire smoke mixed in with his shampoo. If only we didn't have to move for the rest of the night. I'd be perfectly content right where I am.

"How about I grab my swim trunks and we go down to the lake together. Just us." He pulls away, eyes twinkling with hope.

"A different area from where Rick and his flavor of the week are, right?"

He laughs. "Definitely. Come on." He drags me back to camp and the rest of the group is right where we left them, gathered around the fire, telling stories. They've moved on from the last one, not paying us any mind.

"I'm going to walk ahead," I say, before parting ways with Nate at the tent. I quickly pass the drunk, hollering idiots, staying in all the lit up areas as I walk onto the path leading to the water. Crossing over a small bridge, I stop halfway at the sound of a high-pitched scream.

"Wait," a familiar voice says through the trees behind me. Nate. Stomach lurching, I pound my fists against my thighs as I stomp toward the shouting voices. Gabe has Nate pinned to a tree, Nate squirming beneath his hold and pounding his fists against Gabe's muscular chest. Despite Nate's eagerness to get away, Gabe doesn't let up, sliding his hand up Nate's shirt.

"I thought you said you liked me."

"Please, let me go. I'm supposed to meet my brother at the lake," Nate protests and Gabe laughs, undoing the tie on Nate's swim trunks. "I'll let you go once we're done. You want this too. I know you do."

Gabe is bigger than me, his muscles and large build are usually intimidating, but him ignoring Nate's objection triggers something fearless inside me. Marching forward, I grab him by the neck and yank him back so hard he loses balance and lands on his ass. "What the fuck, asshole," he spits.

"He told you to let him go."

"This is none of your fucking business. If he really wanted to, he could've gotten away. Right, baby?" Gabe shoots Nate a pleading look.

"Don't fucking talk to him." Turning to Nate, I cup his face with my hands, lowering my face a little. "You okay?"

Nodding, his bottom lip curls in a little. Fingers grab at my shirt, forcing me to turn around, and I dodge the fist coming toward me by ducking my head. Gabe groans when his hand is met with the tree and all it does is anger him more. He tries to hit me again so I grab his wrist and twist it so hard he screams in agony, something snapping under his skin.

"What the fuck did you do that for?" He clutches his arm to his chest. "I think you broke it."

"Good. You should probably leave and get that looked at."

"You know what? He's not even worth all this trouble." His jaw clenches and he rushes off through the trees, heading back to camp.

"You sure you're okay?" I ask again, reaching for Nate's shoulder, peering deep into his shiny eyes.

"Yeah. I am now. Let's go swimming."

"You sure you don't want to head back or leave?"

"We aren't going to let them ruin our trip, remember? And we can go after we see the lake."

He knows this is how he can get me to go in the water, and he's not one to miss an opportunity. Not when it's being handed to him on a silver platter.

"Okay, lead the way."

Smiling softly, he's already looking more like his usual happy-go-lucky self. People keep trying to take that from him but I won't let them. Fingers wrapped tightly around my hand, he drags me to the lake. The water is black, with a golden hue reflecting back from a large lamp standing tall over the dock.

Stepping closer to the edge, he shimmies out of his shirt and jumps, disappearing into the lake for way longer than I'm comfortable with. Then bubbles rise to the top, followed by a wet, smiling Nate. This is the him I love seeing—free, and like he's standing on top of the world. Ready to be there with him, I kick off my flip flops, lower myself on the deck, and dip my feet in.

"Come closer," he says, swimming back a little.

"You know I can't swim for shit."

"Hold on to the deck when you get in."

"What about when I can't?"

"Then hold on to me." His shiny lips part and before I know it, I'm dunking my whole lower half in, keeping my hand on the withering wood. Cold water stabs at my skin and the darkness surrounding my waist has my heart jumping in my throat.

"I'm right here. Look at me," Nate says quietly, swimming closer. As if waiting for the perfect moment, fireflies loop around us, lighting up Nate's face. Leave it to light to follow him everywhere he goes, and as long as he's here, I'll always have enough of it to help me find my way out of dark places.

He reaches out his hands and I take one at a time, slowly peeling myself off the dock. I grab on tighter when I start to sink and he laughs, wrapping his arms around my waist. "Better?" His lips are so close I can smell his cherry chapstick. It takes everything in me not to stick my tongue out for a quick taste.

"Yeah." I looked out for him earlier and he's paying me back by doing the same. "You sure you're okay?"

"Yeah. I seem to have a knack for attracting all the jerks, huh? I told him he could kiss me and then he decided to take things too far. It's stupid of me to think any of these guys would be willing to go at my pace and care about my needs as much as their own."

"Nah, you're not the stupid one. They are. They're the ones who miss out in the end. Just because they aren't what you need them to be, doesn't mean you won't find someone who is."

"Yeah, and maybe I already have. I just keep looking in the wrong place."

I freeze when he swipes a thumb over my bottom lip. "You'd always stop if I needed to. Put me first and consider my feelings. You'd make sure everything was good for me too. Wouldn't you?"

"I . . ." I stumble on my words, nodding solemnly. "Of course."

"Then you should have been the one to do it."

"Do what?" My breaths quicken, my chest expanding.

"Give me the best first kiss I've always dreamed of. You still can. I'll pretend you were the only one I've ever let try."

Before I can open my mouth to speak again, he presses his lips to mine, his warm tongue slowly pushing its way into my mouth. I slide a hand into his hair, intensifying the kiss, and he leans into me, sweeping in faster and deeper than before. We could be sinking and I'd never notice, my heart soaring above the water enough for the rest of me. We both pull away, gasping for air, and he presses his nose to mine, smiling. "Thanks for always being what I need, whenever I need it."

Does this mean he only needs me in this way right now? Will this be the last time I'll feel his lips on mine? Experience the taste of him lingering on my tongue? Will he eventually find someone who gives him more than I can? So many questions swim in my head, leaving me nauseated. Maybe it's better I don't know the answers. If I avoid them for as long as possible, I can pretend he's finally mine for a little longer.

Deciding it's better to say nothing, I rest my head against his, running a hand down his back. He rubs his lips over mine, breathing in deeply, until loud voices in the distance have me jerking away.

"We uh... should head back now." If we keep going I'll get too used to this, and I can't let that happen or else I'll want his mouth all the time, and eventually more.

"But I like it out here." He pouts, holding me in place.

"I don't think we're going to be alone for much longer, and if we do plan on heading back home tonight, we should leave before it gets too late."

"Then we'll stay, and leave first thing in the morning." He rubs his nose over mine. "Will you stay in here with me a little longer?"

I hesitate, and when he tugs me closer to his body, I sigh in defeat. He really does feel too good to pull away from a second time. "If you don't leave the water, then neither will I."

Humming happily, he kicks his legs and drags me further out into the lake, then lets me go. Panic rises in me when he backs away, but I relax the moment I realize my feet can touch the bottom. "You told me it was too deep for us to stand in."

Looking smug, he swims closer to me again. "No, you assumed, and I just suggested that you hold on to something if it made you feel better."

"Uh-huh." Smiling, I rest my hands on his waist, spinning him around. "Ever dance with someone in the water before?"

"Not until now. It would be a lot better if we had some music, though." Lifting one of my hands in the air, he sways us side to side, humming a song I recognize. I join in, singing the words, and we keep going in circles until we're both falling back in the water laughing.

Loud voices get closer and other people jump into the water, invading our perfect moment. I climb out after Nate and we walk back to camp, dripping wet and shivering. Only one person is left sitting by the fire, wrapped in a blanket and dozing off in the chair. We quietly sneak by him and crawl into our tent. Using one hand to turn on a small night light, Nate hands me a towel and strips out of his trunks with no warning.

He's so beautiful and I don't need much light at all to see that. Unable to tear my eyes away, I watch him until he has on a pair of dry pajamas. "You going to get changed, or what? You're getting our sleeping area wet."

Hiking a shoulder up, I smirk. "I was waiting to make sure you didn't need help first."

Snorting, he turns away as I change into a clean pair of joggers, not bothering with a shirt. I crawl into my sleeping bag and Nate scoots closer to me, turning around so our eyes meet. "How about we tell our own stories before bed?"

"I suck at storytelling," I admit, and he laughs, undoing his sleeping bag enough to grab my hand.

"I'll start then."

"You'll finish too," I say pointedly, and that earns me an eye roll.

He goes on about some ghost in a haunted mansion, but before he can start another story he yawns, his eyes partially closing.

"I think someone's all storied out for the night."

"Yeah." He unzips his sleeping bag all the way down and then mine to snuggle closer to me. His warmth calls to me and I wrap my arms around his waist, burying my nose in his hair. We've never cuddled like this before, but we've also never kissed either. I don't mind any of it. I'll just sit back and let him take the wheel, move at his pace, and hope we always go forward instead of back.

Six

JACE

"You awake?" Soft fingers stroke my cheek, and when I open my eyes, they're met with a pair of sparkling blue ones.

"I am now." Yawning, I stretch my arms behind my head, my hands crashing against the back of the tent.

"Do you think Gabe will tell anyone?"

"What do you mean?"

He puffs out a long breath, dead-eyeing me. "You know what I mean. You probably sprained the guy's wrist. You're not supposed to get in trouble for me anymore, remember?"

"I told you I wouldn't for the remainder of the school year. Never said anything about after." Besides, I'd rather get in trouble defending what's right than for doing something for the wrong reasons. All those assholes deserved more than they got, especially Gabe. I regret none of it. Hopefully he learns to keep his hands to himself from here on out. The rude awakening he got last night could possibly prevent him from hurting someone else. Too bad my father never got that. If only he was stopped before going too far during his first offense.

"I knew you'd somehow loophole your way around things."

"It's going to be fine. I doubt he'll say shit, otherwise everyone will know what he did to cause it."

"I hope you're right." He rolls onto his back, looking up at the shadow of branches showing up on the tent's plastic, light from the sun shining around it.

Resting my hand on his, I squeeze his fingers, giving him a hard smile. "I am. Ready to get out of here?"

"Yeah. Breakfast tacos on the way home?"

"I'll never say no to tacos or breakfast, especially if you're paying."

Huffing out a laugh, he lets go of my hand and sits up, reaching for his bag. "Only because you paid for all the camping gear." It was my surprise to him when he was stressed over finals. I didn't want him worrying about more than he already was and knew the sudden gifts would distract him.

"I'm kidding. I don't expect you to pay me back for that." Tossing the top of my sleeping bag to the side, I crawl toward my clothes and grab a shirt.

"Then don't look at it as me paying you back." He switches his lightning-bug pajama pants for a pair of navy basketball shorts before throwing on a sleeveless gray ribbed shirt. We get older every year but so much stays the same, and I'm worried that when it does change, it'll take what we have with it. "Just see it as me wanting to take care of you like you do me," he adds.

After packing our stuff and rolling up our sleeping bags, we crawl out of the tent one by one, the morning light forcing me to shield my eyes. Chirping and laughter surrounds us as we load the car, stickers latching themselves to the edges of my flip-flops. Two people are at the picnic table chowing down on pop tarts and fruit, while everyone else appears to still be sleeping.

"You two heading out?" one of the guys, I think his name is Andy, asks.

"Yup. Something came up at home and we need to get back early," Nate responds, barely glancing his way, shoving the folded tent on top of his duffel.

"That sucks. We'll definitely miss you," Layla says, staring in the direction of Nate only. Of course she only means him. She and I have barely exchanged more than two words. Didn't matter how many times she came over to our house to study or joined us on our trips downtown to the movies, it was like she was alone with Nate each time, and I felt the exact same as her no matter who else was with us. He's all I care about. The only one I want to be near.

Nate says bye one last time before joining me in the car. We talk about how we should spend the rest of the summer, and he mentions that we could continue camping in our back yard, in the old tree house we used to sneak away to when neither of us could sleep to read comic books and play card games.

"Do you think that thing could even hold us both anymore?" I glance his way and he keeps his eyes on the road.

"I know it's been holding you well." He smiles, giving me a side look.

"What do you mean?" I play dumb, leaning my elbow on the car window.

"Don't think I don't see you go out there sometimes. Why do you?"

Sighing, I look toward the moving trees. "Because sometimes I feel trapped inside the house, within all those walls, and too close . . . too close to below ground. So I go somewhere higher, outside, to remind myself I'm free."

He shoots me a smile, slowing the car as we reach our favorite taqueria. "Then tonight, you can take me high up with you."

"Okay, but don't blame me if we crash through the floor."

He laughs, pulling up into the drive-through. "Good thing Dad has really neglected the grass out there. Should make for some nice cushioning."

We order way more tacos than we can eat in one sitting, taking the rest home for our parents. The guilt from overeating doesn't sink in until Nate has to leave me alone to shower. I don't think about rules as much when he's around, sometimes not at all, and those rare days are when I feel like all the weight has fallen off me. When I'm with him, it's okay to laugh too loudly, run too fast, talk too much, and have fun. It's okay to be whatever I want and say no. Then he leaves, and I'm struck in the chest with a heavy blow of my own fists, needing to punish myself in order to move on. I don't know any other way.

"Aren't you going to shower? I can smell the lake on you from here," Nate teases me from the doorway, dressed in cargo shorts and a teal tank.

"I don't know. Kind of want to keep the scent on me. It adds to the camping experience." I wink, standing up from my desk chair, and he tosses a towel at me.

"Go wash the stink off you and I'll go set everything up."

"You're serious about the tree house."

"I am." His lips stretch into a smile and he spins around, heading down the hall.

Not wanting to keep him waiting too long, I enter the bathroom and reach for a nail file in one of the drawers. I press the blade into my stomach, creating a small cut and drawing blood. I keep going until the guilt goes away. Once the tightness in my chest loosens enough and I no longer see in the mirror what my dad saw, I undress and hop in the shower, scrubbing my body as soon as my feet touch the tub.

Looking away from the blood flowing away down the drain, I wash my hair and my skin, and once they're both free of suds, I shut off the water and dry off. Walking into my room in nothing but a towel, I approach my closet and grab a random pair of jeans and a band T-shirt. Nate's outside, climbing down the ladder with a satisfied grin on his face when I walk out the back door.

"Anything I can do to help?"

He looks back at me smugly. "Nope. Got it all taken care of myself. Wanna come see?"

"Sure," I say, falling victim to his infectious smile. I follow him up the ladder, the wood only shaking a little when I climb into the tree house after him. Blankets are laid out with pillows on top, and Nate's laptop is in a corner next to a box of snacks and an ice chest. Flashlights and a radio rest on the other side of the blankets.

"You've thought of everything."

"Yup. And if I forgot anything, it's only a short walk to the house."

"I guess that's one perk to camping in your own back yard."

"That and the privacy," he adds. "Ever wonder what it's like to make out in a tree house?" He nibbles on his bottom lip, sliding closer to me.

My breath catches in my throat as his face inches closer.

"I . . . I didn't really get to see what kissing you was like earlier," he whispers. "I mean, we were kind of rushed, and it was very short. I'd like to take my time. Only if you're okay with it, that is."

My heart thuds and I nod, stroking his cheek. "It's not about me being okay, it's . . . Isn't it wrong?"

"Did it feel wrong? It's not like we're blood related, and no one will even know but us. It's just a little kissing. Friends do it all the time."

Friends. Man, what a total punch in the gut that is. "Nothing ever feels wrong with you," I breathe out. Maybe this isn't something I should do, but I really want to, and nothing's ever called to me more. This isn't hurting anyone and we both want it. And like he said—and I've told myself many times—we aren't blood related. So why should it be such a big deal?

His eyes brighten and he leans in further, swiping his tongue over his lips. "You can say no if you really don't want to."

I run a hand through his hair, smashing my mouth to his. Lips as soft as yesterday, they leave behind a tingling sensation on mine. Our tongues collide and I pull him closer, thrusting faster into his mouth, mimicking what I've seen in movies. But I don't even really need to. It's like our bodies know what to do on their own, our breaths becoming one as our teeth clash from the growing desperation.

Light spreads from him to me and I feel like I'm being wrapped in sunshine. Warmth fills my heart, and when we finally break apart, I desperately want to go back for more. He could have had this with anyone, but he chose me, and the thought of him sharing it with anyone else leaves a sick feeling in my gut.

"So . . . what do you think? Get a better idea now?"

His nose twitches and he shies away from me, cheeks tinting a pretty pink. "Kinda. May need just a little longer. You know, so I can get a really good feel for it. A little practice never hurt either." His lips attack mine again, our kisses more ravenous, and it isn't until the hardness in his shorts is rubbing over mine that I realize he's straddling my lap, his legs wrapped tightly around my waist like I'm a lifeline.

Melting against him, I explore more of his tongue, tasting as much of him as I can, my hands roaming down his back and ass. He moans into my mouth, our tongues hot and hungry. This is our third kiss and yet it feels like the first. I can't get enough of him, needing more, sneaking my fingers up his shirt, the contact of our skin creating burning electricity.

He backs away, gasping for air, resting his forehead to mine and then laughing. "I think we should kiss more times . . ." He runs fingers through his hair, finishing his thought. "You know, throughout the day, to see if it's like that every time."

"I'm happy to be your guinea pig whenever you need me to," I say, sounding hopeful.

"I'm happy to take full advantage." He has a glint in his eyes as he presses a quick kiss to my cheek, and my lips are feeling jealous. It's crazy. He's still kissing me. Only not in the right place.

"Should we play a game?"

I scoot back toward the pillows and stretch out my legs. "Sure."

Excitement sparkling in his eyes, he reaches for a small yellow box and takes out a stack of cards. The game we play is one we haven't played before, and we spend the next two hours laughing and smiling. I'm glad he decided to continue our camping trip here, resuming right where we left off.

When our stomachs start making noises and the snacks aren't enough to hold us over anymore, he reaches into the cooler and hands me a Lunchable, setting a second in his own lap.

Laughing, I peel back the plastic. "What are we, ten?"

"Hey," he says pointedly. "You're never too old for Lunchables. Just like you're never too old for card games."

"Sure, I guess." What do I know about what ages you're supposed to do all these things anyway? I skipped my whole childhood, basically, living the life my father mapped out for me—one a kid should never have to experience.

Sauce drips down Nate's face and I swipe it away with my thumb, rubbing it off on my jeans. "You forgot napkins."

"There's always something," he says between chuckles, taking another bite of his small pizza. "But that's what I have you for. You make a great napkin."

Smiling, I go back to munching on crackers and ham. I don't mind cleaning up after his messes. I could do it all day. As long as that means he's here with me and not with some asshole like Gabe or Rick.

Two Lunchables and several boxes of Yoo-hoo later, Nate turns on a movie, positioning his laptop next to me on top of a pillow. Snuggling close, he rests his head on my chest, turning to his side. Halfway through the slasher film, he presses his lips to my chin, his kisses trailing to my lips, and we make out until the credits roll, both flushed and breathless.

"Now I see why people like making out at drive-ins and theaters."

I laugh and he kisses me again, slowly and gently this time, his smile pressing to mine. The tree house holds us up for longer than I had expected it to, lasting through two more movies, dinner, and more experimental kissing.

In the morning I expect it all to end, that he won't need to try kissing out for size anymore. I expect him to be ready to explore with someone else with how much more confident he seemed before we went to sleep, but I'm wrong. I wake up to more kisses, and his lips find mine again after breakfast and in between more games in the tree house. Our mouths connect again in the hot tub in the back yard, his hands clinging to my shoulders, and it's hard not to tug him onto my lap again.

I look forward to him reaching for me whenever he needs more of his fix, but by the next day he's stopped, and though I hope it will only be a short break, it turns into the end of what we'd been doing. He'd sworn it wasn't wrong as long as we both wanted it, but if he doesn't want it anymore and I still do, does that make it wrong now?

Seven

NATE

I'm not supposed to like kissing my stepbrother so much, but I lost control of myself, and it was so easy to reach for him whenever my lips tingled with need. I told myself I was only practicing so I didn't suck when it happened for real, but all those times with him felt like more than what they were supposed to. Our parents almost walked in on us several times and that's when it kicked in. This really is wrong, isn't it?

Maybe it was something we could come back from at first, but I let it go too far, wanting more, my body seeking out other places of his, and that was dangerous. No, we aren't blood related, but we're still brothers. If we have to sneak around and hide behind walls, then clearly we're doing something we shouldn't. I keep reminding myself of that fact every time he smiles at me. Every time we're only inches apart. Every time my heart picks up when he looks at me, expecting me to do more than hug him goodbye or hello.

We go on like we always have before the day at the lake—only hugs and fists bumps, with neither feeling like enough. How were they ever enough before? How can I go back to before I kissed him? Before he permanently imprinted his lips on mine. I'm driving myself crazy thinking of ways to prevent us from being alone for too long without it becoming too obvious. I'm not doing this because I want to. It's because I have to. He doesn't bring it up and neither do I.

If we got caught, he'd take the blame. He'd get in trouble. Not me. I see the way my parents eye him with concern when we leave the house together. They still don't trust him, treating him like he's some dangerous wild animal like everyone in town claims. None of these assholes know him like I do. They can pretend all they want, but only I get the pleasure of experiencing all that is Jace.

Sure, he makes mistakes. Who the hell doesn't? His father was born a bad person and tried to pass that on to someone else, but Jace isn't like him. He realized how wrong everything was around him the older he got. Nothing inside him was built to be evil. He's not, and that's a hill I'll gladly die on a thousand times over. It's not other people I worry about him hurting—it's himself. I've seen the cuts and bruises. He says he doesn't know where they came from, but I do, and I try to hide every sharp object I find and hold his hands to keep them distracted.

It's not enough. I want to do more. If only he'd tell me what I can do to make him stop hurting and stop screaming in his sleep. On really bad nights he winds up in the closet, and I have to resist the urge to follow him in there and wrap my arms around him to let him know everything's okay. But I want him to feel like it is too, not just hear it.

Loud footsteps behind me pull me from my reverie. When I turn around, Jace is dressed in his favorite hoodie paired with jeans and pink Vans. I bought him those shoes for Christmas, telling him he needed a little color with his outfits. I didn't think he'd wear them but he puts them on every day.

"Hey," he says, grabbing the bread from my hand to pull out two slices.

"Hey. Where've you been hiding?" As if I wasn't doing the same. It was probably as intentional for him as it was for me.

"Outside raking leaves like Dad asked. I'm about to head to work in an hour. Picked up an extra shift at the restaurant."

"Oh . . . cool." I smear peanut butter on the back of each slice and he does the same, putting everything away as soon as he's done. He's the clean and tidy one out of the two of us, never able to leave behind a mess for too long. It's like he does it on autopilot, not realizing he's picking up after himself and organizing the shelves as he puts things back. I'm guessing it was something expected of him before.

"You doing anything today?"

I shrug, smooshing my two pieces of bread between my fingers. "Yeah. Meeting Layla at the mall."

"Fun. Who's all going?"

"Just us and her brother Michael."

He lifts a brow, his sandwich paused at his lips. "The one who keeps asking you out?"

"Yeah." I blush. "That's the one." Maybe today will be the day I say yes. If I keep my lips occupied with his then I won't have to keep thinking about Jace's so much. A lot of guys find me attractive but there are always whispers around Jace about how hot or sexy he is. The bad-boy vibe he carries only adds to the appeal, and girls often flock around him until they realize who he is.

Not Starla, though. She lives across the street and uses every opportunity she has to talk to him, but I don't think he realizes she likes him. I'm not sure these kinds of things are obvious to him. They certainly are to me, and when I bring her up he laughs it off, shaking his head.

"If you think she's cute, you should go for it," I usually say.

Not anymore. Not after . . . I grit my teeth, avoiding eye contact when Jace looks from his sandwich to me again. Not after I caught her touching him every time she pretended to check the mail over the last few days and I started getting jealous. I don't want to care, but I do. My skin grows uncomfortable and a wave of nausea washes over me whenever I see them smiling at each other.

"So is this like some double date?" His voice echoes around the kitchen.

I bite into my food, shaking my head, and using the peanut butter sticking to the roof of my mouth as an excuse for taking a long time to answer. "No. We're just all hanging out and doing some shopping. I need some new swim trunks and sunglasses."

"Well, who knows, maybe you can put all that kissing practice to good use afterwards." He lowers his gaze at me and a piece of bread hangs in my throat a little too long, nearly causing me to choke.

"Yeah, maybe." I study his blank expression, waiting for it to change the longer he thinks about what I said, but it never does.

Instead, he responds with, "I better get going before I'm late. I have to catch the bus today and the next one comes in ten minutes."

"I can give you a ride, if you want?"

"Nah. That's okay." He finishes off the remainder of his sandwich and walks to the fridge to grab a soda, but only takes a sip before he puts it back. One of the rules, I assume. I try not to ask too many questions because I know he gets that enough from everyone else—our parents, his therapist, neighbors, and whoever else spots any of his weird habits. "Don't want to make you late for your date," he bites out, snatching his phone from the counter.

Is he jealous? Does he not want me to go? I'd stay if he asked me—show up to his work and order food until his shift ends. I do that sometimes, eating my weight in cheesecake.

"It's not a date," I remind him.

Walking past me, he pauses halfway to the front door and looks back. "If you think he's cute, you should go for it." His eyes bore into mine and then he's exiting the house, slamming the door behind him. I sit here for a long time staring after him, trying to figure out if he meant those words or not. I did when I used to say them, but stopped when they no longer felt right.

What did they feel like to him when they exited his mouth?

Not wanting to sit here all day driving myself crazy over the answer, I text Layla, telling her to meet me at the mall an hour early.

Eight

JACE

If I could go back in time and retract my words, I would. I'd acted out of anger and confusion. Was I jealous? I never liked any of the guys he pursued while in school but this feeling is different, comparable to a thousand knots squeezing around my heart. Would he take my advice? It was what he'd told me once, and that was the first thing that popped into my head right after he said maybe to my suggestion while holding eye contact with me.

Was he trying to get a rise out of me or was he simply sending me a message? Either way, my blood feels like it's on fucking fire every time I think about where he is. With Mike . . . or Matt . . . whatever that asshole's name is. He's probably the better choice though. No one will ever be good enough for him in my eyes, but they'd all be more ideal than me. They could give him normal, not only sometimes but all the time. They wouldn't have to try so hard either.

I toss the trash out, taking a deep breath before walking back inside the orange-brick building. Walking without paying attention to where I'm going almost leads to me knocking a tray out of someone's hand, and even after I apologize she glares at me, shaking her head.

I need to stop thinking about Nate and that other guy, but no matter how much I try to keep myself busy with work, I can't seem to shift focus. Maybe it wouldn't bother me as much if he wasn't also avoiding me and pretending to be too tired to watch movies with me or play card games. Why would he do this? Why give me so many good things, only to take them away.

My nightmares are worse too, replacing the dreams of him kissing me—I've put the idea of that happening again far from my mind after so many days since it last happened. I'm more restless than usual, feeling the rules I break rip at my skin even harder, and I listened to my music loudly in my room this morning to drown out my thoughts. It would have disrupted the whole house—disturbed our guests in the basement—except we don't have any guests.

I close my eyes and open them again, slamming my palm to my forehead before rushing to the break room. There's no basement either, because my parents had it blocked off after the last time I fell down the stairs while I was sleep walking. I woke in a straight panic, kicking and screaming before balling up in the corner, crying. I didn't speak for a week after that, and slept with furniture stacked against the door.

Opening the fridge, the can of Coke I popped the tab on when I first arrived at work mocks me. I'd never been allowed to have it before, so I've slowly been letting myself believe it's okay. Then that strong taste hits the back of my tongue, my brain lighting up like an alarm bell, and all I feel is shame. I went behind my dad's back again.

"Why can't you ever do anything right? Following simple rules shouldn't be so hard. You're despicable. A sorry excuse for a son."

His words claw their way inside me, remaining there until I'm back home and able to go to the bathroom and reach for the nail file again. Only, it's not where I last left it so I rush to my mom's bedroom, looking for anything sharp I can find. My eyes light up when I find her sewing kit under the bed. I quickly grab one of the needles, my dad's voice getting louder and ringing in my ears until I finally slide the sharp point along my upper pec. I press and drag until my dad's scolding disappears and his ghost is no longer looming over me.

My eyes squeeze shut and I drop the needle to the ground, tears building in the corners of my eyes. I'm crying from being haunted, not the pain—I barely feel that anymore. I just keep needing more in order for my head to go quiet again. The slamming of the front door has me freezing in panic, and once I can move again I pocket the needle and put everything back how I found it, cleaning up the mess I made before slowly peeking out into the hall.

Nate is humming, grabbing something from the fridge and heading to his room with two small bags on his arm. He doesn't notice me because I don't come out until his door is shut. I hover outside it for a long time with my knuckles unable to come in full contact with the wood. My heart feels like it wants to escape my chest every time I try to knock and I finally give up, walking to my room.

As I'm tucking the needle under my mattress, I hear a loud whimper, followed by what sounds like a scream. Not wasting another minute or letting my pounding heart stop me this time, I rush into the hallway and push open his door. His gaze lands on me, his hand freezing under his covers, and I swear I go into some type of paralyzed state when I see what's on the TV.

Two men are on top of each other, one rubbing his cock over the other's, both dripping and straining. My breaths stutter and he swallows hard, throat bobbing.

"I thought you were hurting or . . . shit, I'm sorry for barging in. I heard a scream and . . ." I scrub a hand over my face, my words catching in my throat.

His jaw twitches and a blush spreads from his face down to his neck. "I . . . sorry. It was, uh . . . the TV. I'm okay. I didn't realize anyone was home."

"What are you watching?" I look from him back to the two ravenous men on the screen going at it like fucking rabbits, one flipping the other onto his back and shoving his cock in him in one thrust. I've been curious before too, browsing porn on the internet, though it never did much for me, but something about catching him watching it has heat rushing to my groin.

"I think it's obvious," he muses, resting his hand above the blanket.

"You often wait for everyone to leave to watch porn alone?"

His lips twitch, chest rising and falling heavily. "No . . . I mean sometimes, but not like every time."

"Can I watch with you?" I point to the empty spot on his bed and his mouth opens before closing again.

He looks at the screen again and nods. "Yeah, okay."

I ease forward and his eyes stay on me the whole time as I slide under the covers. I don't have to look down to know he's naked. His shorts and shirt are discarded on the floor beside him, the bare skin of his hip brushing over my hand as he shifts in bed.

"Jace." His voice rises to a higher octave.

"Shh. I'm trying to watch." I look ahead, sliding my hand under the blanket to rest it on his thigh. His whole body shakes and he releases a drawn-out breath.

"Is this what you wanted to do with that guy today?" I ask, moving my fingers closer to his inner thigh, and he shudders.

"No."

"You clearly want to do it with someone. When you imagine yourself as one of the guys on the screen, who's the other one? Who's touching you and making your thighs shake?"

"Jace . . . I . . . this is crazy.'

"Answer the question, baby brother." I brush the tip of my pinky over his cock head, sparks dancing between us. His eyes fall back in his head, his lithe body arching.

"You," he says almost too quietly.

"I can't hear you." My lips press to his ear and I blow along the skin of his neck.

"You, Jace. It's you I see. It's always you."

I wrap my fingers around his cock, loving the feel of his skin against mine, and stroke him slowly. He jerks forward, moaning softly. "You don't have to pretend today. I'm right here."

I don't know what's come over me but I really have become one of the men in the video, taking charge and making the first move. Unable to resist the way his body responds to me, I continue driving him crazy with my hand, palming his cock fast. Kicking his feet forward, he reaches for my shirt and I tug him away, not wanting him to see the evidence of what I just did.

I don't care what anyone else thinks of me, or how they see me, but I'd rather hide my worst sides from him for as long as I can. "You're so perfect, you know that? From the inside out."

"Can I touch you too?" he asks.

"This is about making you feel good, not me. You're the one who needs this right now." And I need you, I want to say, but I lock the words in my throat, not ready to be so vulnerable and honest. Not ready to put everything out there only to not have the sentiment returned.

"Touching you would make me feel good too." His face flushes and he pants, thrusting into my hand, chasing everything I'm offering him.

"Next time, okay?"

"Okay." He doesn't push me or look back at the TV. We keep our eyes on each other and he grabs onto my face, shoving his tongue in my mouth and lazily dragging it over mine. His desperate sounds vibrate over my tongue and mouth, slipping inside me. Every part of him owns me at this moment. His lips. His pleasure. Especially those fingers tugging at my hair as he shakes from his orgasm.

His mouth stills against mine, warm breath brushing my lips as he presses his head to mine. Laughter spills from him and he kisses me again. This time it's slow and lazy, his nose gently rolling over mine as his hand falls down to my chest, fingers clinging to the fabric of my shirt. "We shouldn't have done that."

"Do you wish we could take it back?" I run my fingers through his hair, slowly releasing his softening cock.

He shakes his head. "No. Not for one second. Do you?"

I trace the seam of his swollen lips with my thumb. "Not for one second. I feel like I was always meant to be pulled to you in this way and I'm tired of fighting it."

"Does this mean you think I'm cute then?" His eyes crinkle in humor, lips stretching into a grin.

"Yup, and that's why I went for it."

We both laugh, laying in bed for a little longer, turning off the movie and kissing some more. As soon as we hear the honking sound from my mom locking her car doors we break apart, and Nate grabs his clothes from the floor, running to our shared bathroom.

"Boys? You home?" My mom shouts from the living room.

I rush past Nate, smiling as he wipes the cum from his stomach, and make my way to my room. Straightening out my clothes, I open my door and stick out my head. "Yeah. We're in our rooms. Nate's showering, I think."

"Have y'all eaten anything?"

"Not yet, why?"

"How about we order some pizza then?" A smile plays on her lips.

"Sounds good to me. I'm sure Nate's hungry too. Is Dad going to be home soon?"

"Yeah. He said he's an hour away. "Have y'all changed your minds about joining us at your aunt's new lake house this weekend, or do y'all still plan to stay home?"

I didn't know Nate had opted to stay home. Neither of us ever cared for Aunt Tracy and her spoiled-rotten kids, and don't get me started on her spineless husband. "I still plan to stay here if that's okay. You know she doesn't really want me there."

"And she knows you're our son and a part of this family as much as the rest of us. Besides, she promised to behave herself, and you boys will be too busy swimming. You'll barely be inside the house long enough to notice any of us."

"It's okay, Mom. Really. I have plans to catch a local band playing downtown this Saturday."

"Okay. I know you boys can be trusted to be here alone for a whole weekend. Y'all are grown-ups after all."

"Don't worry, there won't be any parties, and we promise not to burn the place down." There might be more of me barging into my brother's room when I hear him moan again, though. He keeps finding new ways to lure me in. To make me run to him.

She laughs, plucking her phone from her purse. "I was just really hoping we could get away as a family."

"Next time. Whenever it's not at Aunt Tracy's house."

Chuckling, she shakes her head. "I'll tell your dad we'll have to plan a trip to the beach or something."

My heart lights up. The beach is still something I've yet to cross off my to-do list. I remember being so obsessed with movies that took place on the water, and my dad shutting them off when he felt they distracted me too much from my duties. "I won't say no to the beach."

"Good. Now go back to doing whatever you were doing and I'll order the pizza."

Just as she presses the phone to her ear, I disappear into my room and Nate exits the bathroom with a towel wrapped around his waist. "What's for dinner?" He leans against the frame, eyes glazed over.

"Pizza."

"And breadsticks?" He perks up.

"I guess we'll see. She should know to include them by now, though."

Nate spurts out a laugh, inching closer to me. "After dinner, you wanna watch another movie with me?" He reaches for my hand and my heart flutters.

"Are movie nights permanently reinstated from here on out?"

He smirks. "Yeah. I think they are."

"Does this mean no more dates with Matty?"

"It's Michael, and it was never a date."

"What's even happening with us?" My voice wavers as his front presses to mine, his cock already growing hard again as his lips brush over my chin.

"Looks like we're going for it."

Nine

NATE

So apparently kissing my stepbrother was a gateway move to letting him jerk me off. Today I'm being led further down the rabbit hole, and I'll go wherever he wants me to as long as he keeps fingering me and touching my cock at the same time. After days of sneaking in kisses and listening for our parents' cars, we finally have the house to ourselves for three days, and I wasted no time turning on another porno and moaning as loud as my lungs would allow. Once my mom and dad left for their trip, there was nothing in this world that was going to keep me from getting more of him.

"The more of you I have, the more I want, little brother." He adds a second finger, slathering more lube inside me, and my toes curl. One year apart isn't that big a difference in age, but something about him calling me that sends a fever through me. Yeah, I know it's twisted, but I can't control how my body responds to his sensual tone and the dominance radiating off him. It also sends a strange rush through me whenever he reminds me how forbidden and taboo this is. And they say I should be worried about him. Someone may have to lock me up because I don't think I'm able to come anymore without my stepbrother getting me there.

And boy does he take his sweet time, slowing down his thrusts to an agonizing pace, his fingers occasionally stopping when I'm about to spill right over the edge. He's dragging this out for as long as he can. I'm left feeling both frustrated and more alive than I ever have before. This summer was supposed to be spent with innocent hangouts at the movies and drinking too much at parties, not like this. But here we are, doing so many things we shouldn't do, and with no intentions of slowing down anytime soon.

"Your sounds are so damn pretty. I love seeing you like this, all flushed and falling apart from my hands."

"Fuck, Jace. Stop being an asshole and let me come already."

His face turns to stone and his hand drops from my throbbing cock, his fingers still inside my trembling channel. "Not sure I should after how you just spoke to me."

Where is this coming from? This confidence rolling off him. The cockiness and demanding tone. He takes charge so well when we're alone like this, not backing down when I beg and cry out. I need more of this side of him. He looks so free too. Free of his burdens, self doubts, and fears. This is his game and I'm merely a chess piece he can move anywhere he pleases. He gets to set the rules and not worry about breaking them.

"Please," I beg, my body feeling like it's being tugged in different directions all at once when he starts driving me crazy with both hands again. He adds another finger, and it's like a bolt of electricity strikes me from the inside when he rubs over my sweet spot on repeat.

"Go ahead and come for me, and never forget who took you there. Who can do it again and again so easily if you beg prettily enough."

Holy fuckballs. Now I see what the big deal is—what everyone raves about. Why so many people love being fucked. This is the opposite of suffocating and walls closing in. This is breathing for the first time and being free from restrictions.

It's as earth-shattering as they say—world tilting and riveting. He hits me there harder and I close my eyes, the lights in the room traveling behind my eyelids, creating colorful shooting rays. I'm lighting up inside, and gripped so tightly by pleasure my whole body tenses as I spurt cum all over the sheets, my ass pressing back against his hand.

Turning around, I reach for the zipper on his pants but he moves my hand to his face, his lips attacking mine. Moaning into my mouth, he runs his fingers down my crack and I don't ever want to be anywhere else. Then it dawns on me. He's trying to distract me from getting him off again and it was working. Pressing my hand to his chest, I force distance between us, my heart rate climbing higher.

"Why do you keep doing that?"

"What?" He plays dumb, sweeping loose strands of hair from my face, and there he goes trying to change direction again, but my mind comes right back to the question at hand.

"Why won't you let me do the same for you?"

"Because this is about you, not me."

"Can't it be about both of us?" My voice cracks.

"I don't deserve to feel good." The corners of his lips squeeze tight.

My heart hurts at the tortured look on his face. He really believes that, doesn't he? "What? Why would you say that?"

"Because I've broken so many rules already. I didn't stay in my room last night. I ate candy before breakfast and showered for too long, wasting too much water." He means when he showered with me. I hopped in after him yesterday the moment we were alone in the house, grabbing the loofah and washing his body from behind. Tensing up, he held my hands still and turned around, grabbing the loofah from my hands. It went from me trying to clean him to him scrubbing me in all the places that had my knees buckling.

He didn't bother to hide his scars from me then, but he did keep forcing my eyes onto his every time I tried to look down, my gaze trailing over all his damaged skin.

I cup his face in my hands. "Oh, baby. None of those are bad things. We all do them, and there were two of us so technically we saved on water." I press a kiss to the corner of his lips. "And I gave you the candy, so if I get to be rewarded for it then you do too." Moving my hands slowly down his body, I undo his pants, and he doesn't stop me this time.

His breaths quicken and his eyes are dark with arousal as I reach into his underwear, my cock stirring again when my hand comes in contact with the soft sleeve of skin. He's uncut and fucking perfect. Tugging his underwear halfway down his hips, I lift his dick over the waistband, pushing back the skin and sliding down in the bed until my face is met with his groin. I've never done this before, but hopefully I've watched enough people do it in videos to figure it out. Either way, Jace won't judge me, he never does, always glancing at me with eyes of wonder like he is in this moment.

Licking my lips and the shiny precum dribbling from his tip, I roll his foreskin back and forward, stroking him slowly. I lick at his swollen head, tasting him one inch at a time until he's fully in my mouth, his salty taste hitting the back of my throat. Bobbing my head, I add a little suction, swirling my tongue as I gag a little from his rolling hips.

His eyes are closed when I look up at him, head tilted back as he moves with my mouth, his cock dragging over my tongue, and my throat restricts around him when he reaches the back of it again. I tug at him, enough to draw out another moan, and he pulls at my hair, writhing between me and the bed. "You look so good like this too. Fuck, you look good doing anything really." He releases a hearty laugh.

I release myself from him with a pop, kissing his tip as I catch my breath and smile up at him. "And you taste so good. I want to do this to you all the time, to show you how much you deserve good things."

"I already have them just by having you in the room with me, and I don't even deserve it."

"You do, and you deserve this." I kiss his tip, trailing my lips up and down the underside of his cock. "And this." I lightly suckle at his fat head and he arches his hips. "That too, and definitely this." Sliding my mouth all the way down his shaft again, I move my mouth a little faster this time, burying my face in his pubes while holding my breath for too long. I let him hold me in place, taking what I want him to have, and his pleasure spills down my throat as he comes on a groan.

Letting go of my hair, he goes slack underneath me, and I rub my wet lips along his inner thigh, swallowing all of him down like a thirsty man wandering in a desert. His breaths are heavy pants, slowing down the longer we lay this way, and then he tenses.

"Oh fuck, Nate. I'm sorry. I didn't hurt you, did I?" He lifts his head, stroking my cheek, and I smile up at him.

"No. I mean, my throat may be sore for the next few days but I'll enjoy carrying the reminder with me."

I crawl up his body and press my mouth to his, soaking up the dreamy look on his face—those blissed-out, dark brown eyes, and the black hair sticking to his forehead. Rewards look good on him.

He strokes my neck, smiling dopily down at me. "You didn't have to do that, you know."

"Yeah, I did, and I can't wait to show you how okay it is to drink your next full can of Coke."

A chuckle breaches his lips and his mouth hovers over mine. "You're lucky my brain is too fried for me to argue with you right now."

"Is that all it is?" I like to think it's a cover-up for the fact that he enjoyed what happened so much he forgot about needing to be punished. Otherwise we're back where we started, and he's not ready to remember that he didn't suffer the consequences for all the bad he thinks he did yesterday or today. I'm not either, and I'll do my best to make him forget for as long as I can.

My head is groggy when I wake up, and Jace is missing from my bed. My heart quickly falls into my stomach after realizing what he probably left to do. He didn't get his punishments earlier. What if he woke up thinking he needed them all over again? With panic thrumming in my tight chest, I run out of my room, and a heavy weight shallows my breaths when I don't find him in his room or the living room. A cheesy, savory smell hits my nose and I follow it to the kitchen, smiling from ear to ear when I spot him dancing in front of the stove.

Hips shaking and head bobbing from side to side, he flips food with a spatula. His tone is off-pitch as he sings the lyrics to a song I sang in choir in senior year.

"When did you wake up?"

His body stiffens and he slowly whirls his head. "Oh, you're up. Right on time too, I'm almost finished with dinner . . . and not long."

"Smells delicious." My stomach rumbles louder the closer I get. "What you cooking?"

"Grilled cheese sandwiches and tomato soup."

"Sounds perfect." Realizing I'm still completely naked, I grab his jacket hanging on the chair to drape over my lap as I lower myself into the seat.

"It's something quick and easy," he says, carrying the food over to the table, one plate after the other. I'm already chowing down on a sandwich by the time he sits beside me and pulls his food closer.

"So, Layla invited me over to her house for karaoke night. She promised only a handful of people would be there. Wanna go?"

His shoulders lift slightly and he sets his food back down. "I don't know. I'd much rather finish off this can of Coke and see what happens when I do." His brows waggle and I laugh.

"You know . . ." I slide my chair closer to his, moving one of his hands under the jacket and between my legs. "I think I like your idea better too."

Those first brushes of his fingers are enough to send me into overdrive, and I'm practically turning to goo in my chair when he latches his mouth around one of my nipples, tossing the jacket to the ground. I'm his reward, and he shows me this by the way he touches me—with kisses trailing my body and fingers pressing to my pucker. Lifting me up onto the table, he lays me back, grabs my thighs, and shoves his face between my cheeks. His hot tongue lapping at my seam and fingers tugging on my cock confuses my body about what direction to move in.

Settling on both, I roll my hips, tingles licking at my skin with each dart of his tongue. He goes from slow to fast, feasting on me like a damn second breakfast. I never knew this could feel so good, and was too self-conscious to fully enjoy it at first, no longer caring when the sensation spreads over me like hot lava. I arch my hips, fucking into his hand before pressing my ass to his face, chasing his hungry tongue.

I'm okay with being the center of attention right now because I can tell by his moans and the vibrations of his mouth that he's getting as much from this as I am. Then he does something I don't expect. With a low growl, he zips down his pants, sliding his jeans and underwear down in one swoop. Pinning me to the table, his cock grinds over mine, his tongue driving into my mouth. His hips move too fast for mine to keep up, skin rubbing over skin, his fingers tightening around both of us. Built-up pleasure explodes inside me the more we rub together, his cock head sweeping harder against mine. I combust, cum spurting between us, and he doesn't stop using me to get off until he's covering me with his own release.

Eyes bloodshot, his mouth lolls, and there's that goofy smile I love so much. "Fuck, that was good."

"Yeah," I rasp, smearing our cum together on my skin, and he grabs hold of my wrists, guiding my hand to his mouth. My breath hitches as he licks at my fingers, his tongue swirling over each one to collect every drop, tasting us together.

When we're both able to feel our legs again, he helps me off the table and we shower together. We spend the majority of it holding each other under the warm spray, and he finally lets me wash him, holding his breath while I run the washcloth over his last cut. It's nearly healed, meaning it's been days since he's done it. Wanting to keep the streak going, I keep the rewards coming for the rest of the day and night.

I explore his body with my mouth after we go for a walk for hours outside, rewarding him for getting some much needed exercise. We share another joined hand job, me doing the brunt of the work this round, after we binge a whole season of *Dawson's Creek*. The night ends with us cuddling on the couch and playing Mario Kart.

Staying up late warrants another reward, and I know he's already gotten it in a different way when he can't stop laughing. His smiles stay with me as I close my eyes, snuggling closer to his chest. My breaths even out with his and no nightmares wake him during the night. I wish I could offer him peaceful sleep like this all the time.

Ten

JACE

Ice cream drips down Nate's chin and it takes all my resistance to keep me from hopping over the table to swipe it up with my tongue. Trying to remind myself we aren't alone and all walls are down out here, I push a napkin toward him. "You got a little bit of white stuff right here." I tap my chin.

His cheeks tint a pretty pink and he quickly swipes the napkin over his face, dropping his spoon into the cup. "Not that I mind having white stuff on my face, but this isn't exactly the right kind or the right place," he says quietly, leaning forward.

That earns him a laugh from me and I shake my head, lifting my spoon to my mouth. I asked for three scoops today, instead of my usual one, Nate convincing me that's good because I'm supporting a local business and helping keep them open. His pros always outweigh the cons with the way he words things. Enjoying two Cokes a day is okay because it prevents Dad going into a sugar-induced coma, and eating second helpings of Mom's food means it's less she has to put away in color-coded Tupperware.

Tossing a gummy bear into his mouth, he rests his face on his closed fist, the sun from outside making his freckles more prominent. He really is my favorite view, no matter where we are. He'll point out how beautiful our surroundings are, and I'll only agree because he's standing in the center of it all. The best sight to wake up to is him, with his light brown hair mussed, sleep lines on his face, and long lashes touching his pale cheeks. He's been sneaking into my room through our shared bathroom for weeks now. After a long day, I curl up under my covers, my instincts to hide in the closet nowhere to be found as I wait for his warm body to press against mine.

I stay in bed because he's there, and I'm here around all these other people for the same reason.

"So, wanna go to Barton Springs after this? Take a dip in the water and let me remind you why you love swimming with me?"

My smile mimics his, and not because I'm trying to copy him but because everything he does is so damn infectious, passing right along to me without me always realizing. "What about the drive-in?"

"That's not until later tonight, and you love the water. Well, you love watching it. Being in it is so much better."

"I don't know. That's too many public places in one day. Are you sure you're going to be able to keep your hands off me?" I quirk a brow." Everyone we know will probably be there."

He rests both elbows on the table, running a foot over mine. "We can always go to the dog park area. Hardly anyone goes there. Mostly old people."

I snort. "As fun as swimming in dog piss and slobber sounds, I don't know if I'm in the mood to feel like Jack and Rose from the Titanic. It never matters how hot it is outside, that water's freezing."

He rolls his eyes, slurping the remaining ice cream from his spoon. "Fine. How about somewhere more remote instead, but still with water? I mean, small fish sometimes nibble at your feet, but that's the price you pay when you're so picky."

I bark out a laugh. "Where is this remote place? And don't tell me it's somewhere you've been with Rick or Gabe."

"No. Actually it's where my mom used to take us for family picnics and walks. You know, before she met her new husband and moved to a whole different state to start a new family."

As much as I know his mom's absence has bothered him, he doesn't talk about it often, but when he does, I listen. It's one of the things I've become good at after trying to run in the opposite direction from how I was raised. All the men I ignored and turned my back on as a child suffered and ended up in worse places than our basement. In worse hands than my dad's.

"You had a lot of happy memories there together?" I ask, trying to quiet the thoughts in my head.

"Yeah. At least, I thought so at the time. It wasn't until the last time we went that I really noticed the strain between her and my dad. They didn't love each other anymore and that's fine, you know, but I didn't think it would lead to her no longer loving me."

Lips turning down, I reach for his hand, not giving a fuck who sees. He needs this. He needs me. Not only as a listening ear but as a means of comfort. The tension in his face lessens, confirming the small move is helping. "I'm sure that's not the case. Sometimes parents have a shit way of showing they care but that doesn't mean they don't." I was referring to my own mom. Only her.

"Yeah, maybe." He nibbles at his bottom lip, squeezing my fingers. "Sorry. I didn't mean to be such a damn Debbie Downer on our first date."

My eyes widen, my heart making a strange pitter-patter sound. "This is a date?"

A blush runs over his cheeks and he glances down at our joined hands. "I mean, it feels like one."

My heart smiles and I stroke the inside of his palm with my thumb, tracing an invisible star. "Then it is. And if you really want to go swimming, then we will."

His eyes brighten. "So you'll let me take you there?"

"Yeah. Sure. Why not? How far away is it?"

"That's the thing." His face contorts. "We can't walk there. We have to drive. It's about twenty minutes away."

A knot lodges in my throat and he winces. I look down and yank my hand back in mortification when I realize my nails were digging into his skin.

"Or we can just forget it altogether. There's also a swimming pool that . . ."

"We'll go." I give him a gentle smile. "I want to go there with you."

"You sure?" His eyebrows shoot up and he's wearing a look of uncertainty on his face. "I don't ever want to make you feel like you have to do anything you don't want to."

Not wanting to do all these things with him has never been the problem, and I want to show him they aren't. "I'm sure, little brother. Will you please share your favorite spot with me?" He doesn't have to say what the place means to him for me to know. It's a fond memory he wants to relive with me, and I'd love to recreate with him.

His eyes soften. "Okay. We can grab our bathing suits and towels from the house on the way there."

"Don't you still have towels in the car from the lake trip? Ones we never used because you forgot to get them out?"

"Yeah, but we can't get into the water fully dressed."

"Who says we have to?" My lips pull into a tight grin and his turn up ever so slightly.

"Yeah, I guess you're right."

Shooting up from his seat first, he tosses his trash in the bin by the front door, holding it open for me to follow his actions. We stroll down the road, heading for our house, our arms knocking together, and as soon as we're in front of the garage, he drags me inside and pins me to the nearest wall. Smashing his lips to mine, his hand slides between us, groping my cock.

"Keep doing that and the only place we'll be going right now is inside and upstairs," I murmur against his lips.

"We'll have plenty of chances to do that later. I want to kiss you in places other than this house first."

Liking the sound of that too, I push him toward the car, glancing around us. "Let's make that happen then."

"Lets." Jingling his keys, he gives me one quick peck on the lips before slipping into the car. I follow suit, focusing on his excitement instead of being in a place I was never allowed in.

"Cars are for picking up our guests and delivering them to their new homes. That's all. They aren't for joy rides." My dad's words sting my ears and I tug on my seatbelt, more at ease when Nate slides his hand into mine.

"It's not too late to change your mind."

I shake my head quickly, forcing a smile. "No. I'd rather connect riding in a car to you than to him. I don't want to keep letting his words and memories hold me back from things."

"I don't want that for you either. The asshole stole so much from you. Let me help you take it back." His smile is warm, settling something alight inside me.

We're mostly quiet on the long drive, listening to music and occasionally singing along to the songs playing. We stop to grab food and I tell him to order me the same as him, but it's not until the bag is resting in my lap that the scent of curly fries has my stomach rolling. My fists ball around the top of the paper sack, my breaths painful as they push their way past my lips.

"Feed me a fry, will you?" Nate says, but I'm too far into this state of paralysis to fully take in his words, my body stiff against the seat as I clench my teeth.

"Jace?" He shakes my shoulder, pulling into the nearest parking space. "What's happening? Is it the car? We can get out and walk around for a bit."

I shake my head frantically, staring down at the food in my lap, needing it away from me as fast as possible but not remembering how to use my hands.

"What is it then?" Panic causes his words to shake. "Tell me what's wrong, baby." He pulls at my chin, those blue eyes resembling clouds in a storm.

"The food."

He takes one look at where my gaze is falling and quickly grabs the bag, tossing it outside, no fucking questions asked. The windows roll down and the air already feels less heavy and thick.

"Better?"

My lips press tightly together and I nod, finally able to breathe solely through my nose, the scent no longer strong enough to make my head spin.

"Want to talk about it? Only if you want." His fingers are so soft against my cheek. I lean in closer, closing my eyes and allowing myself to land in my safe place. Nate is a fluffy cloud in a world full of sharp knives and teeth. One I'm afraid I'll end up draining so much, he'll no longer be able to float.

"I . . . That was a reward." It's funny, I didn't think anything was worse than breaking the rules, until I was reminded of my dad's rewards when I made him proud.

"A reward?"

"Yeah . . . he never called it that, but I can tell that's what he meant it as." One of those good memories I was talking about, until they no longer were. "For after I . . ." I swallow the thickness in my throat. "After someone made it to their new home safely. I didn't know the name of the restaurant, he didn't tell me. He'd just hand me a plate with the food already unwrapped. But it was the same place, I remember the smell. He was a manager somewhere, that's all I know, and he'd smell of grease when he got home from work. I think it was his cover job."

Nate's eyes sink, misting over. "Oh, Jace. I'm so sorry. If I had known—"

"How could you? Even I forgot. I've been trying to shove those days down as far as they'll go." Everything forced down is meant to come back up eventually, though.

"I just . . . I hate for this to be linked to today. Maybe we can go home and have a do-over, and I can do better tomorrow. Maybe—"

I press my fingers to his lips, hating that he feels like he's to blame. "I don't want a do-over, baby. I want this right here, with you. It's my favorite way to move forward. You did nothing wrong. I'm the one ruining our day together."

"No, you're not. These are just small bumps in the road while we're moving forward. We can try to make them less rocky, though. How about tacos?"

A smile slowly spreads across my face, and how is he so damn perfect? Because they really are small bumps in the road when he's traveling with me, and I feel like over time I really could crush them until they disintegrate into nothing.

"Tacos sound perfect."

The light returns to his eyes and he steps out of the car to throw the food away in the trash can across the way, distancing it from me along with the awful memory of my dad, leaving Nate as the only thing in my periphery.

When he returns, he immediately starts driving again, turning the music back on and holding my hand. I watch his mouth move around each word of every song, taking in the sunshine bouncing off his cheeks and brightening his smile. His hand moves from my hand to my thigh, sliding closer to my groin, and I'm already looking forward to driving more places with him. How can I not if they all lead to this? To his sneaky, flirty glances at me, and to him massaging my cock with promises of what's to come when we exit this car.

As soon as Nate parks in a discreet area covered by trees, he climbs into my lap, sliding my seat back. Smashing our mouths together, he slips his hands up my shirt, rocking his erection into mine. With drawn-out gasps and pants, we meet each other's thrusts, rutting against one another like two animals in heat. Our clothes restrict us from going too far, and right when I feel as if I could burst at any moment, Nate frees both of our cocks. His soft skin rubs over mine, tiny shock waves of electricity scattering from his skin to mine. The friction is too much and not enough at the same time. Spitting between us, his fingers hook around us and he bounces in my lap, ducking his head as he tugs us both at the same time.

"Fuck," he whispers, lowering his face to mine and sliding down my lap. He releases his grip, and as I'm about to ask what he's doing he presses his head to mine, dragging my foreskin forward. Stretching me around him, he rubs our tips together, and my head spins out of control. The discomfort quickly turns into something world-shattering as he moves his fingers faster, pushing harder into me.

My vision blurs and my balls draw tight. All feeling drains from my legs and arms as I cry out in pleasure. He comes right after me, body convulsing and losing all coordination.

"That was so much better than I thought it would be," he says between chuckles.

"That . . . I was not expecting that."

"I . . . I didn't hurt you, did I?"

My forehead rubs over his and I tuck a strand of hair behind his ear. "Not at all. It felt a little weird at first, but I'm sure you thought that about my fingers too the first time."

"It still feels kinda weird sometimes, but fuck do I love it. I think I'd like your cock too."

I nearly swallow my tongue. "Jesus. Who even are you lately? Such a filthy mouth you've developed."

"Just be glad you're not in my head."

I laugh, pressing a brief kiss to his lips. "I kinda wish I was now. You never have to censor yourself around me."

"No? You might regret saying that soon." He smirks, tucking himself into his pants and sliding back into his seat.

"Let me be the judge of that." I zip up my own pants after wiping myself off the best I can with napkins from the food bags.

He hands me some wipes from his glove box to clean my hands after he's done, then we grab everything we need from the car, including the food, and start our short hike to what he says is the best spot here. Many rocks and a short trail later, we reach a waterfall, and Nate lays out our towels. We eat, watching the water, and somehow it manages to be both loud and quiet, the splashing and splattering sounds mixing with a gentle breeze of wind.

I'm really glad he chose to come out here rather than return to the house. He was right about us not needing walls to kiss and hold hands. Out here we're free in all ways. I don't feel trapped or suffocated and I can reach for Nate whenever I want. No limitations. The best of both worlds. A group of people join us by the water, before floating out on inner tubes and paying us zero attention.

They don't know who we are, so can't hold any kind of judgment, and it's nice to finally get to enjoy kissing Nate around others—for what we have to be as real to them as it is to me. I'm not making this up. This isn't some dream. Nate's not only mine to me and him, he's mine in their eyes too. We're not just some dirty little secret out here.

His fingers tugging at mine drag me from my thoughts. "Come swimming with me."

Without another thought, I let him guide me forward, the cold water shocking to my skin at first. Shivering next to me, he pulls me deeper, our feet still touching the bottom when we reach a small waterfall. Looking from me to the steady stream, he smiles. "Want to go under with me?"

With my gaze following his, I hesitate for a moment, and then say, "Yeah. Might as well while we're here, right?"

He squeezes my hand tighter, taking a deep breath. "On the count of three, then. You can't let go of me no matter what, though, okay?"

"I wouldn't dream of it."

"One," he calls out, keeping his eyes on me. "Two." His chest moves quickly, his nails poking into my palm. "Three." He rushes forward and I hold my breath, tightening my grip on his hand as we're submerged in water. The heavy pressure squeezes me at first, cold and pricking at my skin, then just as it gets to be too much he steps back, tugging me with him, and we both gasp for air. Laughing, he gives his hair a shake, droplets going everywhere, and I duck, still holding his hand. I hold it as he spins us around in the water, while he takes us back under the fall, and when he's ready to lay out in the super-shallow end.

Head tilted back and face flushed, he closes his eyes, soaking up the sun's warmth, and I lean in closer to him. He's my sun, and the risk of being burned from getting too close has never been more tempting. People come and go while we stay where we are, chatting about nothing and everything at once.

"If you could pick anywhere in the world to go, where would it be?" He opens his eyes, flashing me a smile.

"Here." I tug him closer to me, nearly pulling him into my lap and he snorts.

"No. Really. The sky's the limit. Money isn't an issue and you can literally visit anywhere for an entire week."

I twist my lips, pretending to give it more thought. "Still here."

"Is that your final answer?"

"Yes. Right here and right now."

"Then it's mine too."

Eleven

JACE

"You should pay attention to the movie. We can't keep coming back to see the same one," Nate says, tilting his neck away from my ravenous mouth. I don't listen, and just continue to lose myself in the taste of his skin, licking along the pulsing vein in his neck.

"Jace. The movie."

I shake my head, nipping my way to his mouth. Our tongues seek out one another, increasing the hunger we both share, and the movie on the screen falls away with the rest of the world. His hand tugs at the front of my shirt, his teeth knocking against mine. Our breaths are heated, mouths sloppy and wet.

Gasping for air, we break away and I kiss the tip of his nose, stroking his cheek. "You know I didn't come out here with you for the movie."

"No? Why not stay home then?"

"Because I want this with you everywhere I can have it." I press a chaste kiss to his mouth.

"Luckily there will be so many other places. We'll be hours away from here soon, sharing an apartment off campus together." He strokes my fingers lazily, his face beaming in the small light the bright screen brings.

"We will. But people will learn who we are to each other eventually. I don't know if you've noticed, but I can't seem to break away from my name." Or the darkness lingering in me. I've kept it mostly at bay here, but what if I lose control and forget the right way to love him?

"You will. Everyone there will know you the way I do. They'll see what I see, not your name or your past. Not everyone is small-minded like most of the dipshits in this town."

"Yeah, maybe. But sometimes I think you see only what you want to see when you look at me."

His eyes lock on mine, fingers sweeping through my hair. "I see all the parts that matter most. None of us are perfect. All of us are winging life and making mistakes along the way."

Normal mistakes. "Yeah, maybe you're right," I say, knowing it's what he needs to hear. What I need to be true. The nightmares are feeling real again, pulling me down into the dark when I feel him slip from my arms in our sleep. What woke me up last time was looking in the mirror and seeing my dad's face underneath layers of dried blood. I sink my teeth into my bottom lip, using the pain as a distraction—a short escape from my torturous thoughts.

"I know I am," he squeaks, wrapping his fingers around mine while shoving popcorn into his mouth.

I kiss him one more time before reverting my attention to the movie. Leaning his head on my shoulder, he jumps when the killer emerges from the curtains, and I wrap my arm tightly around him, laughing when he buries his face in my shirt, shielding his eyes. "Tell me when it's over."

"Why do you always choose a scary movie just to purposely miss all the best parts?" I rub my nose in his hair.

"I'm not missing anything when I can still hear what's happening," he says apprehensively.

I laugh, pressing a kiss to his cheek when he finally lifts his head to look at the screen again. "That's true, but seeing it all is so much more fun." The more memorable the scene, the better. I'd rather think about all the horrors someone else lives through than my own, mostly because theirs aren't real. It's all an act for entertainment purposes. In the end they scrub off their makeup and go home, but I can never leave my movie. I'm forever looking over my shoulder, waiting for the men my father owes to come collect, or for him to get free and drag me back to the basement.

For the cops to decide I'm also guilty and lock me up in a different dark place. For most of our neighbors and others in town to finally convince them it's where I belong. Every time someone is reported missing or is jumped in an alley all eyes point to me. Why would it be anyone else?

This is the curse my father left me with. He damned my future before I could have one. I will forever be his son, the boy who helped his father seal the unwanted, disturbing fates of many who are unable to have a voice ever again. He left me with all this guilt and hatred toward myself. All these what-ifs. What if I'd run out of the house sooner? What if I'd ignored the lies he fed me and listened to all those victims before it was too late for them—before they disappeared forever.

I haven't looked him up in years and he hasn't tried to contact me. At least not to my knowledge. I know he's alive, though. I know because everyone around me can't stop talking about him being up for parole. My mom and dad can't hide it from me forever, and I can't keep avoiding the news either. He might get out some day and I worry what will happen when he asks me to come home. Will who I'm trying to be now tell him where to shove it, or will the scared boy inside me quickly obey?

"Then you can keep being my eyes for me and tell me what you think I've missed," Nate says, bringing me back to him, And I try to stay there, I do, but when he and the movie go quiet my brain works overtime, taking me away to places I wish I could avert my eyes from the way Nate does with scary scenes.

"Look at me, boy," my dad would say. "This is who we are and what we do." His dark eyes grow larger in my head, his hand reaching out the way it did when I was a kid. I shake his image away and pull Nate's hand further into my lap instead, folding my fingers around his so tightly his nails dig into my palm.

I feel the pain they bring, and focus on Nate's glowing eyes as they widen at the scene unfolding on the big screen. I push down harder on his hand until my dad's fading face is nothing but a black hole. Nate looks at me, and as if reading my mind, he drags his nails over the skin of my wrist in soft circles. The sensation is different from pain, tickling a little and slightly gentle, but just as effective. He shows me I don't need punishments to feel better about enjoying life, and I don't need pain to stay with him either. And right now, with his eyes boring into mine, he's saying, *"Look at me. You can be whoever you want . . . do whatever you want."*

And with him right next to me, showing me another way and showing me him, I feel more reassured. He goes back to watching the movie and my gaze bounces between him and the screen. When he hides his face again, I paint him a perfect picture of what's happening, and he continues to remind me what I'm supposed to be doing by creating new sensations on my skin. I'm here on a date, watching a movie and making Nate feel safe from all the monsters on the screen. Because I want to always be who he said I was, and I will be, for him if not for myself.

"Your dad is the nightmare people ran from, and you are the type of person who wakes them up so they can be okay again."

Stroking his cheek and nudging his side, I point to the screen when it's finally safe for him to open his eyes. He moves away from my shoulder, blinking those pretty blues open, and I feel like I really am the person who's made it all okay for him tonight.

"How many more times do you think this guy's gonna pop out?" He holds his hand close to his face, pressing his cheek to my arm.

"You know he can't get through the screen, right?"

"As far as you know." He snaps his eyes to me.

Smiling, I shake my head. "Well, we're also in a car, so if that happens we can always use it to get way ahead of him."

"They always catch up. You know that." He swallows down more popcorn, the scent of butter mixing with his sweet shampoo.

"If he does, you can use me as a shield and I'll tell you when it's safe to lift your head again."

"I doubt that'll work when it comes to real life."

"It will as long I'm here with you. I'll make sure of it."

Nate jumps out of the car first, using a magazine from the back seat to shield his head from the rain, and I rush after him. Droplets of water splash over my face, soaking my hair, and I almost stand still so I can surround myself in it a bit longer. I could if I wanted to. I could stay out here and play in the rain for hours. No one would stop me. I smile, slowing my steps and lifting my arms. Nate looks back at me, the magazine flopping over his head barely holding together.

"What's taking you so long?"

I smile, looking up at the sky and slightly parting my lips. It's so damn freeing—the smell of dew, my shoes scraping over the concrete, and the dark sky opening up above me. All of this is so far away from everything that was in my dad's house, and even further from the cold, grungy basement. Maybe that's why staying is more tempting.

"You're getting wet," he says with a touch of amusement in his voice.

"I know." My lips tilt higher and I reach up, pretending to touch the sky.

"Get your ass inside. You'll trail water onto the carpet," the voice in my head says, and I shake my head to my dad's words, spinning around.

Tossing the magazine onto the sidewalk, Nate rushes my way and grabs my hands. "I guess we're staying outside for a little longer."

I blink down at him, pulling his body closer. "We can go inside if you want. You're getting soaked and starting to shiver."

"So are you. You know, I've always been curious about what it's like to kiss in the rain." He stands on his tiptoes, his mouth so close I can taste the warmth and cinnamon from the pretzel he made us stop for before heading home.

"You don't think it's the same as kissing in the shower?" My breaths mingle with his, my tongue begging to be closer.

"Do you?" He tilts his head, one side of his mouth lifting.

"No. This is nothing at all like being in a tiny space, surrounded by white tile walls and a glass door." I smash my lips to his, loving the cool night breeze wrapping around us and the sky putting on a light show to prove how much better this really is.

When our clothes hang off our bodies and we can hear the water slosh around in our shoes, we rush into the house. Neighbors turning on their porch lights around us have us ducking our heads, laughing as Nate gets the door open with his key. The first inside, he starts stripping in the entryway, kicking off his shorts and shoes once his shirt is off. With his hair dripping and plastered to his skin he smiles, slowly moving toward me in nothing but his white briefs that leave little to the imagination.

They're as wet as the rest of his clothes, making them see-through, but still acting as a barrier between us when he presses his body to mine. He lifts up my arms, pulling off my shirt and tossing it to the ground, and shakes water from his hair. "We're getting water everywhere." He drops his hands from my pants and goes still when his eyes meet mine. Can he hear the raging storm inside my head? Sometimes I feel like he can. It gets so loud it shakes me from the inside, causing the outside to tilt.

Nibbling on his bottom lip, he looks down at the small puddle on the floor and back to me. My jaw tightens and I step back onto the small rug in front of the door, tugging at my pants. Quickly moving forward, he stops me and yanks me closer to the living room. "You know what? It's okay. Water can easily be dried up."

"I'll get a towel," I say quickly, but he holds on tightly to my hands, making it impossible for me to get away.

Shaking his head, he sways back and forth. My shoes leave more wet spots as he drags me around the coffee table. "Tell me what's happening in that head of yours," he whispers.

"A whole lot."

"Too many thoughts spinning out of control?"

I nod curtly, gliding back and forth with him.

"Then let's find something that'll make you focus on the world spinning instead."

With his hands tightening around mine, he pulls me toward a large empty space between the kitchen and living room, spinning me around with him. Putting more space between us, he leans back a little with so much trust in me, moving faster in small circles until we're both falling on our asses and laughing hysterically.

The room still spins as I reach for him, and he reaches for me back, kissing my lips. We're both off balance, sharing more laughs as we try to stand up. I'm the first to fully reach my feet, and once the ground finally feels like it's stopped moving beneath me, I lift him from the floor, yanking him closer to me.

"Better?" he asks, his voice almost too quiet.

"Much," I say, rubbing his smile with my thumb. "So much better."

"Shall we go get dressed for bed?"

I slip my fingers into the back of his underwear. "We should go to bed but skip the being dressed part."

"Okay. Well, let me help you with these then." He helps me out of the rest of my clothes, taking his time and being very gentle. Once I'm in only my underwear, like him, he runs to the bathroom to grab a towel, dries the floor, and leads me to my room. We crawl into bed and he drags the covers over us before curling himself against me. Warmth radiates off him as I wrap my arm around his waist and tuck my leg under his.

He gives me hope that everything will be okay. That I can one day leave all the bad parts of me behind, along with the bad memories. Then I close my eyes and the darkness shatters all my confidence, bringing me closer to everything I hate—everything I fear.

Twelve

NATE

Jace wakes up screaming multiple times throughout the night, and at one point he holds me in place, squeezing me so tight my bones ache under the weight. I can't push him off no matter how hard I try, eventually giving up the fight and going slack in his hands.

"You need to go back," he says. "You can't be here." Tears glisten below his eyes as the sun starts to pour into the room.

"Jace," I say, stroking his cheek. "It's okay. You're dreaming."

"Don't," he screams. "We'll both get in trouble if you fight. Do you want that?"

My heart hurts. I wish I could do more for him at this moment, and eventually my attempts to wake him up have his eyes flying open. Fear is etched in his expression, his body tensing and features strained.

"Jace," I say in a soft voice, kissing his lips as his arms fall away from me. "Are you here with me?"

"I . . ." His bottom lip trembles. "Did I hurt you again?"

Letting out a soft breath, I shake away the pain in my arms that will no doubt spout bruises tomorrow. "No," I lie. He doesn't need more reason to punish himself and he can't control what he does in his sleep. I know what happens when he has nightmares and I stayed anyway. I stayed because he needs me, and because I need him—to feel him breathing and fighting to be here.

"You should go back to sleeping in your own bed. You're not safe in mine." His voice wavers.

"I don't want to. I already told you I'm fine," I exclaim.

He shakes his head, flipping to his back. "I don't like hurting you. I don't like knowing it was me who gave you a black eye or left fingerprint bruises on your neck. I don't—"

I pull his face toward mine. "Look at me. I'm fine. You'll only hurt me if you push me away, so please don't."

His eyes hold on to mine, his throat bobbing. "I don't want to, but I will if it keeps you safe from me."

A heavy weight settles on my chest, a twisting sensation making it hard to breathe. So many people failed him—so damn many—but I won't be another person on that list. "I don't need to be kept safe from you."

He shuts his eyes, takes a breath, and opens them again. Big, brown, and soft. No danger or maliciousness to be found, only worry and sorrow. "I'm not so sure."

"I am." I rub my nose over his, kissing his slanting lips, needing the corners to lift for me again. "Want to tell me what they were about? Maybe talking about what happened will help you feel better."

Muscles jump in his throat as he swallows hard. "It's my dad. I see him and then I become him. I'm the one making someone else drag those people into the basement. I'm the one everyone hides from."

A lump lodges in my throat. "You're not him and he's not you. You were a victim too. He hurt you just as much as he hurt them. If you can come to terms with that while you're awake, then maybe you won't see yourself as anything else in your dreams either."

"He didn't, though. I wasn't sold off like some shiny toy for someone to do what they pleased with. I got a second chance at life, in a good home and a safe environment. What do they get? More torture? Nightmares they can't wake up from? He died, you know."

My eyes widen, heart stopping in my chest. "Who did?"

"The man everyone thought I saved." He sniffs. "He was in a coma for weeks before his family decided to let him go. "He suffered too much head trauma and it was my fault. Our tumble down the stairs. I killed him. I looked it up a few years ago, not sure I wanted to know what happened to him. I needed to know, though."

"Oh, Jace." My heart wrenches, unable to let up when I look deeper into his eyes. So much pain and torment takes over. I never knew the man died. I thought Jace saved him that day too.

"I only saved myself. And for what?"

"No, Jace. You saved the others who would have come after him. Your dad would have kept taking more men home, and now he can't thanks to what you did."

"But what about the men he worked for? They'll keep doing it. They'll hire others. They'll replace my dad and it'll never end. So did I really help anyone? The guy had a family. He . . ." A sob escapes him. "He was supposed to attend prom a month after he was taken. He was younger than I am now."

"You can't keep thinking about all that. You can't. You'll only drive yourself mad."

"I haven't thought about it in a while. Not until I saw him again last night. I . . . I forgot about what I'd done. I forgot like it was nothing. I went on like it was nothing while his parents had to bury him in the ground. I got to be happy and graduate when that was all taken from him by me."

"Tell me what I can do to help you. Tell me what you need."

He shuts his eyes, pulling away. "I don't know. Just sit here with me and talk about something else."

"You want to forget again?"

"No. Just be distracted. To remember that not everything in my life has been bad."

Smiling softly, I sit up against the headboard when he does, taking his hand in mine. "Okay. So have you seen Starla's new haircut? She looks like she stuck her finger in an electric socket."

He snorts and there it is, that little curve of his lips. His face turns, cheek pressed to the cold wood as he strokes the inside of my palm. "Still jealous of the girl next door, huh?"

I roll my eyes, scooting closer until our hips touch. "Nah. She's not the one who gets to be under the covers with you while you're in your underwear."

He barks out a laugh, pressing his forehead to mine. "No she doesn't. That's reserved for you and you alone."

"It better be," I say in a sultry tone. Wanting to pull him further from his nightmares, I trace the seam of his lips with my tongue and slide my hand between his legs. Hiking up my fingers, I brush the tips over his swelling head, only a thin layer of fabric preventing me from touching skin with skin. I need that. I can tell by the needy look in his eyes that he does too.

My mouth claims his, my tongue thrusting between his parting teeth. His fingers gently tug at my hair as he deepens the kiss, tasting more of me, and our heavy breathing turns into desperate pants as I tug on his underwear, yanking them down his hips as he lifts his bottom. I kick them down by our feet and his mouth presses harder to mine, our breaths becoming one.

I take off my underwear next, climbing on top of him and reaching for the lube I tucked away in his drawer. Straddling his lap, I smile against his lips, lifting up my hips to finger myself. I slick up my hole until I'm dripping, spreading myself wider with two fingers.

He pulls his head back, flicking his eyes at me, his hand on my shoulder. "What are you doing?"

A moan escapes my throat as I rub my ass over his stiff cock. "I need you inside me. I want to be as close as I can to you. To feel like we're one."

He licks his lips, stroking my lower back. "You sure?"

"Yeah. I'm sure. Make love to me, Jace. I want all the first times with you I can have. I want all of you, all you're willing to give me."

"Everything," he breathes. "I want to give you everything, baby."

Balancing myself on my knees, I lift up to line his head with my hole. Slowly, I press down, taking him inside me inch by inch. My hole squeezes around him, the tight rings of muscle making a popping sound as he breaches my entrance.

"Fuck. You feel so good. I don't think I can last."

"It's okay. I don't want you to. Come inside me. Make me feel more like yours, big brother."

His eyes darken and he pumps his hips upward, sliding deeper into me, and a slight pain surges inside me as I let out a small gasp.

Bottoming out, he goes still, running his hand up and down my back again. Our skin creates sparks everywhere. A fire cracks between us as we start moving against each other again, my hips slapping down to meet his.

Our lips collide, teeth clashing as we swallow down each other's moans with our hungry mouths. Skin slaps skin as I ride him faster, my cock jolting between us. Hot squelching sounds push me closer to the edge and the discomfort of feeling like I'm being split in two dissolves. Pleasure sprouts through me, so strong it makes my muscles tense. Together we're making the world spin, reminding him there's so much good he can still have, that he's stronger than the nightmares and gets a say in where his mind goes—right here with me.

"That's it. Stay with me. Watch me. Think of me." I bury my face in his neck, rocking my hips and riding the wonderful waves of ecstasy. Reaching between us, he strokes my cock, and more beautiful sensations crawl up my spine. I lift my face, rubbing my cheek over his as I wrap my arms around him. My body goes slack as I let him take over, giving him all the power here.

What happens next is his choice, and I fight back my orgasm, not wanting to come until he's ready for me to.

"You're close, aren't you baby? I can feel that pretty hole locking onto my cock like a vise. Fuck, it's milking me so good."

"So close. Need to come soon. But only when you feel I should. Only when you think I'm ready." He can't always control what goes on in his head, but right now he can control me, and fuck does it feel good letting him.

Flutters erupt in my lower stomach, a heat surging through me the longer I hold back. He edges me with his cock and hand, lips tickling my ear as I wait to hear those magic words. I can feel his lips curl, his warm breath kissing my skin as he bucks his hips.

Sweat gathers between us and he kisses my cheek. "Look at you, flushing a pretty pink. On the verge of tears. You going to cry for me? I was told tears can be a good thing. Can you show me?"

I nod, choking on a breath as he brings me higher into the sky. "It's starting to hurt."

"But you like it, don't you? Hurting you doesn't always have to be bad. I don't mind causing you this kind of pain. Not if it makes you fly and look this damn free."

"Yes. Please don't stop. I need more."

His hand goes still on my cock and he licks at one of my nipples before tugging it with his teeth. I spasm out of control, my balls full and tender.

Fingers moving again, he strokes my shaft slowly, my skin feeling like there's a fever burning me up from the inside.

Hole overly sensitive and cock twitching, tears spring from my eyes. It's too much. All of it. But also everything in the whole world. Who would have thought something so torturous could drive me closer to heaven. The sky is opening up above me, bathing me in light when he says, "Just a little longer. I need you to hold out a little longer for me."

He comes with a low grunt, cock pulsating inside me as he fills me with hot liquid. I squirm, my skin tight and my head light.

Biting at my nipples again, he tightens his fingers around my painful erection. He squeezes around me, loosening his grip as he works his way back up my base. His skin rubs over mine, creating wonderful friction and sensations. Stars appear behind my lids when I shut my eyes, and he parts his lips over my ear. "Come for me."

Letting go of all restraint, I slump against him, coming so hard I temporarily black out. My body feels both overused and restored. The room spins when I open my eyes, his hands creating tingles as he caresses my skin.

"You're so amazing. So perfect. The best kind of good I could ask for."

The door creaks open and we both freeze, my high quickly fading when I hear a loud gasp.

"What the hell is going on here?"

Our mom stands in the doorway, clutching her hand to her chest. Eyes wide and face pale, she steps closer. Her gaze shifts up and down as she takes in our linked, sweaty naked bodies, cum staining our stomachs.

Mortification sets in. No. They aren't supposed to be home until tomorrow. This can't be real, but no blinking or pinching myself takes me away from this dreadful moment. She's not only really here, she's still standing there, looking like she's about to keel over. Jace's eyes blink, his mouth gaping. Say something. Anything.

"I asked you a question. What is this?" Her tone shifts to a higher octave.

I lift the blanket around us, sliding off Jace's lap. "I . . . You're home early."

"Hun, are they up there?" My dad calls up the stairs and my mom's brows lift. She looks behind her, taking a step back into the hallway.

"Yeah," she calls back. "They're watching a movie." Her eyes meet mine again, her face flushed. "Can you get the rest of the bags out of the car? I'm going to get started on lunch."

"Sure thing." His voice fades away as the front door closes with a loud thud.

"I don't know what's going on here, and frankly I don't want to know, but it ends now. Right now. I'm going to leave this room and when I come back up here you both better be in your separate rooms, fully dressed. I don't want your father finding out about this. He has enough to deal with as it is with your grandma in the hospital. That's why we came back early." Her gaze drops to the ground and she slowly slinks away, shutting the door behind her.

Her heavy steps pound against the wood floor and Jace tosses the blankets off him, moving quickly to his dresser. He throws me some clothes and pulls on some blue basketball shorts. Neither of us talk for a long time, the silence loud in the room.

Rubbing the back of his head, he lowers himself onto the bed and holds a graphic tee to his body, his eyes drooping. "I did this," he said. "If it wasn't for me—"

"No," I say with conviction. "You don't get to do that. You don't get to take the blame for what happened. I asked for it."

"That's because it's what you thought I needed." He turns away from me, bunching the shirt sleeves between his fingers.

"I needed it too. Please don't blame yourself . . ." Please don't punish yourself, I want to say, but the words get trapped in my throat. I try to relay the message to him with my eyes, and his face contorts.

"You're the one who keeps hiding all the scissors and sharp objects in the house. You sold all of Mom's good knives in the last garage sale."

"Yeah, and she blamed Dad. You have to admit, it does sound like something he would do," I say humorously, trying to lighten the mood.

"How . . . ?" His eyes grow heavy, his hand bleeding as he digs his nails into his palm.

"All the scars and new cuts you kept getting." I grab his hand, pulling back his fingers. "You don't deserve that. I hate that you feel like you do."

He yanks his hand away at the sound of the front door slamming. "You should go to your room. I'd hate to make her more mad than she already is."

I rub at the blood on one of my fingers from his new wound and stand from the bed. "Yeah, okay. It doesn't mean this is over. It's not. We're not."

He looks away. "Go. Now. Just go."

I open my mouth and close it before exiting the room through our shared bathroom. The distance hurts. I can't stand being so far away from him or the thought of leaving him alone after experiencing a bad moment. I was trying to make him forget they existed for a while and all I did was cause more.

"Lunch is ready," my mom calls.

I hurry down the stairs and Dad's already sitting at the table with a glass of iced tea in his hand. Mom is busying herself around the kitchen, her expression blank, and Jace is nowhere to be found. I sit in the first chair I reach and Mom sets a plate in front of me, her eyes not once meeting mine. Jace comes down almost twenty minutes later wearing a long-sleeve shirt. He's done something he doesn't want me to see. My stomach cramps and I want to run to him, but I can't.

Not with the way Mom's glaring at me from her seat. We eat in mostly awkward silence, my dad the first to break it by talking about their trip being cut short. He mentions going to see my grandma, asking me to go with him, and I nod as I shove another bite of food into my mouth.

"What about you, Jace?" My dad's eyes flit his way.

"I . . . Yeah, okay."

"Actually, Jace can go tomorrow," my mom chimes in. "I need to talk to him about something."

"Oh, alright," my dad says, brows lifting in suspicion. "Everything okay?"

"Yeah. Everything's fine." My mom forces a smile. "We'll all go tomorrow."

Neither of us say another word, and after my mom clears the table my dad and I leave for the hospital. The drive is short and quiet. I look out the window, trying to distract my mind. This can't be the end of us. I won't let it be. I don't care what Mom says, I won't stay away from Jace for long. He's the best kind of good I could ever ask for too . . . even if he can't see it.

Thirteen

JACE

Mom looks down at the table, her face wrinkling, and I can tell she's trying to gather her thoughts. Trying to make sense in her head of what she saw and how to move forward. She scrubs harder at the wood and then falls forward, her face landing in her hands. Her loud sobbing cuts at my chest like a knife. I've disappointed her again. I always will, won't I? I can't keep pretending I can be the son she needs me to be.

"Mom, I—"

"Don't," she says under her breath, rubbing at her eyes. "Just don't."

"I'm sorry. It was my fault, not his. Please don't blame Nate for this."

"I don't." She straightens her back, unable to meet my eyes. "I don't blame you either. It's that man's fault. What he did to you . . . It's my fault. I should have looked harder . . . I should have . . ." She lets out a sigh, shaking her head.

"I love him. I know it's not right, but I do."

"I knew you two spent too much time together. Your dad didn't think so, but I knew." Her voice shakes. "I just knew it wasn't normal. How close you got. All the hugging and hand-holding. And no . . ." She looks me right in the eyes. "It's not right, sweetheart. And it's why I have to make a decision. A hard one."

"What do you mean?"

"You're an adult now so you're old enough to go where you want, but I think you should go stay with your uncle Judd for the rest of the summer."

"What?" My heart stops in my chest. Judd lives in another state, far away from here. I'd never see Nate again. That's why she thinks I should go. She doesn't want me near him. She no longer trusts me.

"I'm sorry but . . . it's not a good idea for you to stay here. Don't think I'm giving up on you because I'm not, but Jace . . . what I saw today." Her hand lifts to her chest and her bottom lip shakes. "What if others found out? What if . . . I don't think anyone else would understand. I mean, I'm trying to myself."

"It won't happen again, I promise. Please don't make me leave."

"It's either that or another group home. You and your brother don't need to be near each other right now. I think he's confused too, and you being here will only make it worse. Time away from each other will be good for you both. I've talked to your uncle already, and he said he could use some help on the farm."

"Mom—"

"Please," she begs, with her eyes as much as her words. My throat closes up, breaths strangled in my lungs. "Do this for him if not for yourself. You both have so much to look forward to, and I'd hate to see you both throw it all away for some strange phase you've fallen into."

"Phase?"

"He's your brother, Jace." Her words shake me up inside, my nose flaring. "Can't you see what you're doing to him? I think you need more help than we realized. You came home too soon. I wanted you here so bad, I didn't want to see it. I can't have both my sons..."

"I'll go." I lower my head, tugging at the hem of my shirt. "You don't have to remind me of all the trouble I've caused since moving here. I'll go."

"Jace." She reaches for my hand and I shove her away.

"I'll go to my room and pack."

She doesn't say anything else, nodding as I rush up the stairs. What do I tell Nate? That I've agreed to leave him so I wouldn't cause him more trouble than I already have? So I wouldn't destroy the full life he could live without me being here? What if all this time away makes him see what everyone else sees? I wouldn't be able to handle him looking at me the way they do.

Slamming the bedroom door behind me, I stare at the photos of us Nate plastered all over my closet mirror. In some we're smiling, and in others Nate is stretching my lips with his fingers. Marching forward, I yank the pictures off the mirror, then gather everything else I plan on taking with me before shoving it all into two bags.

A knock at my door has me jumping back, almost dropping everything. My mom enters, wearing a frown. "I booked you a last-minute flight for tonight. Your uncle will be waiting for you at the airport when you arrive."

"Will I get to say bye to Nate?"

Her eyes are heavy and she shakes her head. "I don't think that's a good idea. He may not understand right now."

I nod, sliding the straps up my arms. "When do we leave then?"

"I can take you now. That way you have time to check in, and just in case we run into any traffic on the way there."

"Yeah, okay." My stomach knots at the thought of leaving without telling Nate how much I love him and how sorry I am for everything. This is the right decision. I know it is. He'll thank me later. I needed this push to protect him from myself. I was unable to walk away without it, and even now I'm struggling.

"Do this for him." My mother's words play in my head as I follow her out the door and load my bags into the trunk.

I will. I'll do it for him. I'd do anything for him. He's always given me what I need and now it's my turn.

I press my cheek to the cold glass window as we pull out of the driveway, and I close my eyes, remembering the moans slipping from his lips earlier. Remembering how good he felt. Remembering how good he tasted. Remembering how I'll never have that again.

Fourteen

NATE

He left me. I didn't want to believe it. As soon as my mom told us he was on a plane on his way to uncle Judd's I ran to his room. His favorite hoodie was missing from the closet. Leftover residue from the tape was stuck to the glass of the mirror where all our pictures last were. Holding my chest and taking painful breaths, I collapse on the bed.

The room blurs out of focus and I lean forward, tears pouring from my eyes. Wretched sounds escape me and a weight rests beside me, a hand rubbing my back.

"It's going to be okay," Mom says, not sounding convinced by her own words. "He'll be back. He's not gone forever."

I sob harder, burying my face in my hands. An ugly sensation spreads through my chest and I can feel myself breaking on the inside. How long will it take him to come back and piece me together? Will there even be anything left by then? I need him back now.

"Why?" I cry. "Why'd you make him leave?" She told my dad it was because she wanted to protect him from Bobby after hearing about him being up for parole. She was worried about his safety, she'd said, but he'd still be joining me at college and we'd have our own place together.

I know the truth, though, and it has nothing to do with his dad. Mom lied. She's going to keep our secret but probably more for her and Dad's benefit than ours.

"It's what's best right now. You two will be okay, I promise. Being out on the farm with the animals could be good for him."

I shake my head and wipe my eyes with the back of my hand. "What if it's not?"

Her eyes narrow and she takes my hands. "It's better than him staying here. Than what was happening between you two. You both need some time without each other is all. Be around other people. Make new friends."

"I have friends, and I meet new people every day." I shove her hands away. "This is only good for you and Dad, not us."

"You can still talk to him on the phone. He's your brother. You two can't . . . It's not right," she whispers.

My throat clogs with emotion and I stand from the bed.

"It's not your choice to decide what's right and not right for me. We aren't actually related. Who cares if we want to be together. We're adults who are free to make our own decisions."

"You don't know what you want right now. You're still both too young. I know he's always been a huge influence on you and—"

Anger burns in my veins. "What? If anything, I've always been the one to suggest things. He was always too scared to take a chance on anything. Jace wouldn't even drink a Coke without punishing himself afterward. Did you know he was cutting? Did you?"

Her brow furrows. "What?"

"He was hurting himself every time he thought he broke a rule. Why do you think so many pairs of scissors, nails files, and razors went missing? It was hard to keep him from everything. He always found something." My gaze shifts to the broken mirror on the dresser.

She slowly stands, her jaw twitching. "You knew all this time?"

"Yeah. I did. He stopped for a while and then today happened." My heart falls further the longer I stare at the shattered glass on the floor, one small piece covered in tiny drops of blood.

Her eyes bulge and she covers her mouth. "I'll have to let your uncle know. I'll call the therapist. I'll—"

"You did this. He was getting better and now who knows how much of that has been undone. This will be another thing he'll always blame himself for. Another reason to feel ashamed and damaged."

"That was never my intention and you know it. He knows we love him. I'll always love him."

"Did you tell him that? He's the one who needs to hear it, not me," I scream, rushing to my room and slamming the door behind me. I haven't said it to him lately either. I'm just as guilty. I reach for my phone, ignoring the knocking on my door. I have nothing left to say to her or Dad. She wants me to leave the house more and to meet new people, then I will. I'll be so busy with all these friends she wants me to make, I won't have time to be home for dinner or family movie night. They'll only see me when I walk through the door and leave the house.

"Nate," my mom calls on the other side of the door. "You'll understand why I'm doing this eventually. You both will. It's not because I don't love either of you. It's because I love you both too much."

Gritting my teeth, I lower myself onto the bed. Feeling like there's a fire in my chest, I rock back and forth, taking in deep breaths. My fingers shake on the phone as I dial Jace's number. No pick-up on the first or even the third ring. I reach his voicemail and hang up to try again. I keep calling, and after the fifth time of the call not going through, I leave him a message. I tell him I love him over and over. I tell him I'll see him soon. I tell him ten good things he's done lately and that he deserves a reward for each one.

One: You kept me from getting scared at the movies.
Two: You made me appreciate the rain more.
Three: You held the door for four people yesterday when we got gas.
Four: You cleaned ice cream off my face.
Five: You paid for the popcorn and pretzels.
Six: You washed the dishes so Mom didn't have to worry about it.
Seven: You offered to take a shift at work so your co-worker could enjoy their birthday.
Eight: You saved me all the orange Starbursts.
Nine: You saved a bee from a puddle.
Ten: You gave me the whole world this morning.

"I love you," I say one last time with a sob catching in my throat.

It's only two months. I can survive without him for two months. But can he survive himself? He's his own worst enemy, especially when the only words he's surrounded by are the ones in his head.

Dropping the phone on the floor, I curl in on myself on my bed, wishing I could sleep the rest of the summer away. My mom's words are tangled webs in my head. I picture Jace alone on the plane, having to be around so many people and experiencing something huge all on his own. I can't stop the worry from seeping in further. My head is on the verge of erupting and I'm the one who needs my world to spin faster than my thoughts for once.

Every night for the next few weeks, I sneak into Jace's room when the rest of the house is sleeping and snuggle under his covers. As his scent begins to fade, so does he. I no longer feel him on his clothes when I wear them. His hoodies are more mine than his now, and when my mom comes into my room to wash them while I'm at my new job, I nearly lose it. Every bit of him that still lingered on the fabric is replaced with detergent. I toss the hoodie forward, falling back onto the ground and punch the floor with my fists. I thought things would get easier, but they haven't. I also hoped he'd respond to messages by now. So far, they've all gone unanswered. Mom says he's busy on the farm and that not every area out there gets service. Does he read them? Does he listen to my voicemails? Does he still laugh at my horrid singing and bad jokes? I've snuck some cheesy farm ones in there on my last call to him.

I hope he reads and hears them all. I need him to know I'm falling apart without him. I need him to know nothing is the same without him here. I also need him to know, this isn't his fault and that he isn't a monster. I tell him all this almost every day through texts, along with long explanations of how all my days are going. I tell him about the parties I pretend to have fun at, how many times I have to fake a smile and all the guys who hit on me who I want nothing to do with because I'll only ever belong to one person. They aren't him. No one is. I tell him about the movies I watch and how hard it is to shield my own eyes from scary scenes. I can't watch horror movies with other people. It feels like I'm trying to find someone to take his place every time I consider it. I can't go swimming with anyone else or have them know about the tree house. That's our secret place and I can't stop stocking it with our favorite snacks or adding more games. Getting to my feet, I stare at myself in the closet mirror and wipe my eyes.

"Nate," Mom calls from the kitchen. "Dinner is ready."

"I'll be down in a bit." I run my fingers through my hair and rush to the bathroom to wash my face until I feel I look decent enough. Mom and Dad are chatting in the kitchen when I walk down. Mom shoves something in her shirt when she notices me approaching the table. She does that a lot lately. What is she hiding? What doesn't she want me to see? Is it something from Jace. The clear worry in her eyes says it can't be.

"What's going on?" I ask, sitting in the chair I always sit in, trying not to stare too closely at the empty one next to me. Trying hard not to imagine him there, reaching for my hand under the table or kicking his feet toward mine.

"Nothing. Just going over bills." She forces a smile, and my dad does a horrible job trying to match it.

"Okay," I say, not bothering to continue my questions since I know the answer won't change. "Hear from Jace today?"

She shakes her head. "No, but he did say he wouldn't be able to talk until later in the day. He's thinking about staying out there the rest of the year now."

What? He can't. We made promises. If he stayed that long, then that means he will miss our first semester of college. "Why would he do that?"

She adjusts her apron, looking at my dad before meeting my gaze again. "I don't know. I think he really likes it. He sounds really good being out there. Happy."

Happy? What even is that anymore? I haven't felt it since before he left, and here he's able to experience the feeling without me. Not that he doesn't deserve to because he does. More than anyone I know. I want that for him. I really do. I'd just prefer it be in our college apartment with me.

"What about school?" I say, hating the obvious desperation in my voice.

"I don't know. He can always join you out there next semester."

"Yeah." I take the plate from her hand, placing it down in front of me. I'd hate to have to wait that long. But if this is something he really needs, then I'll give it to him. I could do that, couldn't I? "I guess he still has two weeks to decide."

And though I want him to choose what's best for him, I still hope he'll pick us. *Pick me. Come back to me.*

Fifteen

JACE

Weeks of working on the farm and I've yet to get used to the smell. Lifting my shirt over my nose, I push the shovel under the horse shit, and when I'm done cleaning out the stalls, I feed all the animals. Getting an early start helps me finish by lunch time. Not wanting me to miss breakfast, my aunt Rachel walks out to the barn to bring me a toaster waffle or biscuits with sausage wrapped in a napkin. She always makes sure I have plenty of water and snacks on me too. I actually like being here.

There's only one thing missing—him. He's been blowing my phone up ever since I first got here, stopping for a few days only to pick up where he left off. As hard as it is not to answer, I let the voicemail get each call. The distance is hard enough as it is, but knowing we'll never get another day in his or my bed together... Knowing there'll be no more sneaking out to the old treehouse or to movies... No more him...

He thinks it's only for the summer, that we'll be together again soon. He's counting down the days and I hate how hopeful he sounds in each message. I want to answer. I want to tell him I love him back. On the days I struggle the most, I read his texts and listen to his voicemails. Closing my eyes, I pretend he's right next to me and speaking into my ear. I can almost smell the sweet candy on his lips again. All the orange Starbursts. He never was able to convince me how good they were until I tasted them on his lips the last week we were together.

If I answer his calls and respond to his messages I know I'll take back my decision. Not going back home is for the best. I won't be gone forever, though, only until I'm sure he's moved on and realizes how much I held him back. Until he realizes he can have a much better life without me. I signed up for community college forty-five minutes away from here, switching my degree to agriculture. I haven't told him I won't be joining him at the university we'd both dreamed of going to together since freshman year. I don't know how to. Hearing the hurt and anger in his voice would cut me way too deep. I'm barely keeping it together as it is, the hole in my heart growing larger every day.

Entering the hen house, I collect the eggs in a bucket and put them up high in the enclosure so the raccoons and other animals won't get them. There's been a huge stray cat problem lately, and too many have managed to sneak past the dogs over the last couple of days. Sweat drips from my brow as I check the electric fences and move the sheep to a new section of the pasture.

Healthy green grass sprouts around my boots as I wait for the last group of lambs to make it over. The smallest one circles my legs, *baaing*. He's bottle fed so not as skittish as the others. I bend down to pet his soft fleece, wiping more sweat from my face with my shirt, and a smile cracks along my lips when the lamb tries to suck on it.

"Not feeding time yet, buddy." I give him one last pat on the head before turning around and closing the gate behind me. Kneeling in the grass, I yank the water bottle from my back pocket and chug it down, allowing my face to soak up the sun.

The farm life is as peaceful as it sounded. Animals truly are better than people. They didn't judge you for your past mistakes or remind you of the ones you made. They rely on you and look forward to your presence. They're gentler and easy to please. I do no wrong out here. I don't hurt Nate in my sleep since I go to bed alone. I don't hurt my mom by always doing the wrong thing, and here I'm not known as the kid whose dad kept men in his basement.

I get to have a new start. It's a second chance. I should be happy and relieved to be far away from all the bad memories—to be away from my dad—but I'm also far away from my best friend, and I still feel like I need him every day. Those smiles. His contagious laugh. His silly lists and random plans for us. He doesn't need me, though.

"Lunch is on the table," Aunt Rachel shouts, and I wave her way to let her know I heard her. Otherwise she'd continue screaming her head off. A slight breeze wraps around me and I stride toward the house, offering my skin some relief from the sun. The summers are hot here but not as hot as in Texas. I didn't mind spending my days out in the sun when Nate was there to jump in the lakes and springs with me. The only water to take a dip in around here are the ponds, though, and there's nothing like fish nibbling at your feet when you go for a quick swim to cool off.

"Just about done for the day?" Rachel swats at a bug and I nod.

"Yeah." I squint when the sun creeps into my eyes too much and I follow her into the house. "I don't have much left to do but I'll get it taken care of after I eat."

"I'm sure you will. You got a phone call while you were out." My aunt and uncle are some of the very few people with a landline. No one ever calls for me on it either, so I'm a bit taken aback by her words.

"Yeah?" I take off my hat, setting it on the hook, and leave my muddy boots by the door.

"Yup. Your brother. He asked me to have you call him back. Wanted to see how you are."

"He has my cell number." I head for the table and my aunt shakes her head, nodding at the sink for me to wash my hands.

Chuckling, I oblige, and she starts talking again.

"Yes, but you aren't answering it. At least he says you aren't. Any particular reason why?"

Why won't you just move on without me Nate? I can't if you can't, and you need to. It's for your own damn good.

Cold water mixes with the soap on my hands, creating suds as I rub them together. "I must be getting them when I don't have service. I haven't seen any come through."

She casts a glance at me, lifting a brow. She's much harder to lie to than my mom and dad were. "Mhm."

"I haven't, Auntie. I swear."

Her lips smack together. "You can keep lying to me all you want but you can't lie to yourself." She points her finger at me, tucking her shirt into her apron. "Now go eat before the food gets cold."

"It's sandwiches," I say, pulling out a chair.

"And I said what I said. Eat." Her eyes harden when she glances out the window. "Where's that uncle of yours?"

"He was out on the tractor," I say, sitting down in front of a plate holding my favorite chips. My aunt was sure to get them during every grocery trip. I'm very spoiled here and I've never once felt like a burden. I think my aunt likes having someone to take care of and my uncle appreciates having cheap help. He talks about me taking over the farm for him someday, saying I was made for it. Maybe he's right. No one's ever had so much confidence in me before. No adult at least.

"He's going to run himself ragged one day by going so dang long without eating or drinking."

"I think he already has," I deadpan, and she laughs, bringing a pitcher of lemonade over to the table.

"You might be right. That man can barely make it through an episode of his favorite show these days, and they're only thirty minutes long."

My uncle loves his true crime. I've caught him listening to podcasts while brushing the horses. Last time we were in the stall together, he took off his headphones and hooked his phone up to a Bluetooth speaker so I could listen too. I fell asleep to one last night, waking up thinking I was being strangled when my wired headphones wrapped themselves around my neck. I hate the wireless earbuds because of how easily they slip out of my ears, but I might come around to them soon.

My aunt talks about the weather and the new sheep my uncle has to pick up tomorrow. I plan on going with him so we can stop by the bookstore on the way because reading on my phone is becoming a chore. I used to share Nate's Kindle with him. I also really miss touching real book pages and enjoy grabbing a tea after my purchase.

"What are you reading these days anyway?" My aunt fiddles with her napkin.

"Thrillers. Suspense." I answer between bites of my food, dabbing my face with a napkin when mustard drips down the corner of my mouth.

"You're turning into your uncle," she laughs.

Smiling around a chip, I nod and reach for my cup. "Yeah. I guess he's rubbing off on me a little." I like having someone who's a good influence to take after. My mom's husband was a good man and treated me well, but we never really bonded over anything. He always seemed worried about saying the wrong thing, tiptoeing around me like he was walking on thin ice. And well, my real dad was no one I ever wanted to model after. What I do in my dreams is not who I am, and I need to keep telling myself that, even though a part of me is scared of being wrong.

"You're not your dad," I remember Nate saying. I might not be able to hold on to him but I can carry his words with me everywhere I go—and I do. Out in the barn, in the pastures, on the tractor, at the bookstore where the coffee shop clerk sometimes flirts with me, and as I fall asleep at night.

"Well, as long as you don't end up as stubborn then I think you'll be just fine." She winks, clearing off the table.

I help her, tossing my trash and setting my dishes in the dishwasher. After I call my uncle to come eat and drink something, I bottle feed the babies and fish in the pond until the sun begins to set. Nate would love it out here. All the large moss trees and the way the sun shines down on the water. He'd lay back beside me on the dock, telling me how beautiful the view is, and all I'd be able to see is him.

I take out my phone, reading over the last messages he sent while I lower my fishing line into the water.

Nate: One of these days you won't be able to ignore me anymore.

Nate: I hope you didn't meet some cute country boy or girl out there, because if you did you better let them know who you'll always belong to.

Nate: Please answer me. At least with a hi.

Nate: I miss you.

My throat goes dry, strong emotions building up in my chest, creating an uncomfortable pressure.

Nate: I love you.

My heart sinks and I trace his words with my fingers, hoping he knows I feel the same. I want to say it back. I do, so fucking bad. It hurts too much. But if I say the words we'll only keep going in circles, hurting each other more when school starts and I don't show up.

He'll always be my favorite kind of good, and I'll always be the bad he can do without.

Sixteen

NATE

Even though we're nearing the end of the semester, I still watch the front door of my small apartment. My parents wanted me on campus after my uncle told them about Jace's decision to stay in Missouri. He didn't tell me though, and I wouldn't let myself believe it was true until I heard the words from him myself. He could change his mind, and if he did, he'd need a place to go. A place with me. Months later and the words still haven't come. My hope is dwindling.

Not once while we've been apart has he written me back or returned my calls. I don't stop sending messages, though. If anything, I've doubled them, attaching pictures of me eating lunch at the nearby park or watching one of our favorite movies. I send him a picture of all the extra space in the tub whenever I take a bath, the extra pancakes I can't finish on my own, the new books I buy for us to buddy read when he gets here.

I want him to know I haven't given up, that I'm still waiting. Waiting for him to wrap his large arms around me in the new king bed I recently got. Waiting for him to sit behind me in the tub to wash my hair. Waiting for him to come here and give me more good deeds to add to our list. Waiting for him to need me to turn a bad memory into a good one. Waiting for him.

Breaking my eyes from the door I decide I'm angry at for never opening and bringing me what I need, I look at the time on my phone. When I realize I only have a short amount of time to get to class, I jump up from the couch and grab my backpack from the floor. Before pocketing my phone, I tap on Jace's name.

Me: I'll save you my chips from Quiznos today. You know I always only want the sandwich and drink.

Me: It's supposed to snow a little today. I heard you got a lot where you are. Hope you're staying warm.

I slide the phone into my pocket and exit the apartment. The weight is so heavy, increasing with every unanswered message. Dragging one foot in front of the other, I pick up the pace when I spot my car, then I get in and drive to school, still waiting for my phone to vibrate. Waiting for Jace to be ready to end the silence between us. Waiting and waiting. Always waiting.

Seventeen

JACE

Lying on the ice-covered grass, I trace the clouds with my fingers and pop another chip into my mouth. The cold sharp shards prick at my skin and I press my arms harder against them. I need to feel something other than the hurt in my heart today. I need to focus on something other than the emptiness and guilt I feel. I left him alone. He hasn't stopped messaging me and I haven't stopped reading everything he sends.

His words are what help me get through the days easier. Sometimes they're random thoughts or jokes he's heard. Sometimes they're book recommendations and new flavors of coke he thinks I should try. Others are "I love you" and "I can't wait until you get here."

Doesn't he get that I'm not coming? I thought he would after all this time. My mom called the other day telling me how good they were all doing and how I should come down for Thanksgiving. The wavering in her voice told me she was still unsure of me being there, that she doesn't trust me. I don't trust myself either. If I go, I won't be able to stop him if he decides to crawl into my bed or join me in the shower. I won't be able to stop my lips from finding his and my fingers from tracing the beauty marks around his nipples. I also won't be able to stop hurting him in my sleep.

The nightmares have gotten worse. I wake up to torn sheets and feathers everywhere. I've broken my headboard and scratched up my face so badly blood was everywhere. I don't know if it's the loneliness or sadness lodged deep inside me, or if it's because I'm not sleeping as much as I should. Maybe they'd come regardless. Maybe they were always meant to take over my dreams. Does that mean they'll take over my life too?

Either way, I won't let them reach him, and in order to ensure that, I have to continue staying away. What if not wanting to be like my dad isn't enough? What if the anger and disgust I feel for people like him will fade over time? My dad was once a good person, wasn't he? My mom wouldn't have married him otherwise, or had a child with him. I don't remember the good side of him but that doesn't mean he never had one.

How old was he when he lost his fight to the darkness? When did his morals and compassion fade? When did the monster take over? Did he not see it coming, like maybe I don't?

My mom got tangled in his loose threads, and when they finally broke it was too late for her to come out untangled. He made it all worse by subjecting me to the mess he made of all the unraveled pieces.

I won't risk doing the same to anyone I love. I won't risk Nate. And that's why I must sacrifice what makes me happy . . . So that he always has a chance to be.

This is his third semester without me and he still won't give up. He's met some new friends and I couldn't help but smile at his horrible choice in bedroom curtains.

I need you to come help me pick better ones. You always had a better eye than me.

His last few messages all started with *I need you.* I lift up my shirt, pressing more of my bare skin to the frigid ice, and close my eyes. My heart hurts every time he begins his messages that way. I want to be there. I've stopped myself from getting into the old pickup truck I bought with my savings, many times. When he got stood up on a blind date. When he got his car broken into. When some guy tried to rob him in the school parking lot, and when he came down with a bad case of the flu.

I wanted to be there so bad. But he has others now. Better options. Safer people in his life who won't corrupt his mind like I did. No, my mom didn't say those exact words, but she implied them. She didn't think I was a good influence on him and she was right. I'm no better now than I was then. I'm still broken and bruised inside with too many inner demons to battle. I'm still in love with my brother. I still want way more with him than I should. I still want him. I still need him too.

Pushing myself up with my hands, I take my phone out of my pocket to do the second hardest thing I've ever done. Sucking in my breath, every muscle tenses inside me as I click on his name, and after reminding myself how much more he needs this than me, I hit the block button.

No more new messages. No updates about his life. No more "I miss you" and "I need you." No more him.

I debate deleting all his messages and pictures as I stride back to the house. I think about it some more when I'm in the shower and putting on fresh clothes for supper. I think about it while I'm eating my aunt's famous roast beef and reading one of the books he told me about out on the back deck under the stars.

Then, when it's time to turn in and I'm lying in bed unable to shake my dad's words and all the men's faces from the basement, I pick up the phone and read Nate's messages. I distract my mind with something good and read them out loud until my thoughts are spinning with him instead of everything else.

That's when I realize I'm not ready to let everything between us go yet. As I'm setting my phone down on the dresser, a loud thud downstairs has me sitting up on high alert. Glass shatters and I get to my feet, with my finger ready to call 911.

"Aunt Rachel? Uncle Judd?"

No one answers. Trying to steady my breathing, I grab a baseball bat from my closet and peek outside my bedroom door. The hallway is dark and quiet. Only my own breathing and soft footsteps surround me. Then there's a high-pitched scream, and when I rush toward it I see a person in a black mask, with their back to me, pointing a knife at my aunt. My uncle is on the ground, passed out with a head wound. With trembling fingers, I quickly hit 911 on my phone, turning the volume all the way down and shoving it back in my pocket.

"Tell me who else is in the house?" the guy with the mask demands.

"No one," she squeaks.

Another guy walks around the living room, tossing everything he assumes is valuable into a black bag. Fear licks at the back of my neck when he looks my way, and I press myself to the wall, trying to hide myself in the dark.

"Did you hear that?" the guy with the bag asks, searching around some more.

"Hear what?"

"I don't know. I thought I heard a noise coming from the hallway."

"Well, don't just stand there like a dang idiot. Go check it out," the first guy says, and I'm assuming he's the one in charge.

"Please don't hurt us," my aunt begs. "Tell me what you're looking for and I'll get it for you. You'll be able to leave a lot quicker if you let me."

"Shut up. Did I ask you? No." His hand cracks across her face and I clench my jaw, tightening my grip on the bat. They weren't expecting me to be here. Do they know my aunt and uncle somehow? I didn't leave the house a lot, and my uncle hasn't been able to talk me into going to church with them yet. He picks up the groceries and everything else in town while I wait in the car.

My aunt falls to the floor, sobbing into her arm as she lands against the cabinets. I wait until the second guy looks away before slipping into the laundry room across the way. As I close the door, I leave a small crack and wait until he walks into the first room he reaches. He's going through the drawers, opening them and slamming them shut when he doesn't find what he's looking for. Knowing he'll be busy in there for a while once he stumbles upon my aunt's jewelry and the cash she hides under the bed, I sneak back out to the hallway.

The first guy is looking down at my aunt, pointing the knife at her necklace. "Take it off or I'll cut your neck to get it."

My heart shoots up into my throat as my aunt reaches for the gold chain with shaky hands. As she turns it around and unclasps the back, the diamond on her engagement ring shines under the light.

"Well ain't that a pretty ring you got there. I was just thinking about proposing to my girl. I think that'll look a lot better on her finger than yours, don't you?"

"Fuck you," I scream, coming at him quickly and striking him in the back of the head with the bat. The wood slams against his cheek first as he attempts to turn around, and I swing again, hitting him so hard in the head I swear I hear a crack. As a scream crawls up his throat and he swings his fists my way, I slam the bat into his knees making him buckle. His body hits the floor like a sack of potatoes, and when he drops his knife I kick it away.

Face covered in blood, his words come out scrambled and he spits out a tooth. He reaches for my aunt and more rage fills me, my hands having a mind of their own as I hit him some more, unable to hear my aunt's pleas for me to stop until the man lies lifeless on the floor. His friend comes rushing out, tugging off his mask. I've seen him before. He's helped load my uncle's groceries before.

"Where the fuck did you come from? What did you do to my brother?" His footsteps toward me come to a halt when sirens blare outside. Backing up, he looks around with panic in his face. "I told him we needed to stop. He didn't listen. Said this was the last one." Muscles tense in his jaw, tears streaming down his cheeks, and when cops barge through the front door, he holds his hands up.

My aunt crawls to my uncle as he comes to, coughing up blood. They've never been through anything like this before. Those assholes weren't wrong about this being their last fucking house. With heavy breathing and heart still beating fast, I drop the bat, and when the cop tries to cuff me, my aunt stops him.

"No. He's our nephew. He lives here and he saved our lives. That man on the floor threatened to slit my throat and could have killed my husband with how badly he beat him. They're the ones you want." She points to the lifeless body on the floor and the man slumping to the ground placing his hands behind his back with large regretful eyes.

He'll be out in a few months, I'm sure. And once he's out, I'll be watching and making sure he doesn't find himself in another similar situation. No telling what they would have done to my aunt and uncle if I wasn't here. I might not be able to stop myself from doing the wrong thing in my dreams, but today I was able to stop others from doing it in real life.

Weeks go by and I find myself in a dark parking lot, stopping a man from forcing a woman into his car against her will. And it doesn't stop there. I start wandering into random bars, and get invites to parties where men try to slip drugs into peoples drinks or get too handsy in some dark corner. It's almost as if the universe is sending these people my way on purpose, or drawing me to the places where they are. Sending them to jail just isn't enough.

I find where they work and get them fired from their jobs. I break up their relationships. Make their lives difficult, forcing them to always watch their backs like they've done to others—wanting them to know what it's like to live their lives in constant fear.

And when I no longer accidentally stumble upon them, I go looking for them, needing more. Needing to teach worse people a lesson. People who deserve the pain and suffering I used to think I did. People who are like my dad. Because if I stop them, they can't hurt anyone. If I stop them, I'm not the monster in my dreams. The more of them I stop, the further I get away from being my dad.

I play his words—*"Make me proud"*—in my head, right before doing the opposite.

Eighteen

NATE

More holidays went by where Jace didn't show. It's Christmas break and he's missing this one too. I expect he'll miss my graduation as well. It's been years. Years of me crying and loving him too much. Years of me needing him to appear out of nowhere and tell me he's back for good. Does he even look the same? Does he have a farmer's tan and toned arms from working out in the pastures daily? No doubt he's as handsome as ever. It was only a matter of time before he'd no longer be able to ignore lingering eyes.

Mom said Jace is seeing someone when I asked about him earlier. Her name is Lindsey and her father purchases hay for his animals from Uncle Judd during the winter when the grass is mostly dead. I felt like my heart was separating from my chest when she told me. I didn't want to believe it at first. Does this mean he'll be staying away for good, or will he be bringing her with him when he finally decides to visit?

Will I be able to handle it? Seeing them together, doing everything we once did? Does he have a hard time keeping his hands off her like he did with me? I clench my eyes shut, taking a breath, needing the images to disappear from my mind. The ones of them together on the farm, holding hands and talking about their shared future.

Opening my eyes, I look down at my phone screen and scroll all my unanswered messages before writing back a guy I recently met at a party. My fingers freeze against the screen and when all I can hear is Jace whispering all the words that were once for only me to someone else, I hit send.

Me: Sure. Dinner sounds great.

Glen: We can pick a time and place when you get back then. See you soon, cutie.

I wince at the nickname and then start to wonder if Jace has one for Lindsey. Does he call her baby too?

The next breath of air I inhale squeezes at my lungs, and I shove my head between my knees as a wave of nausea washes over me. One thing I know for certain, is I'll never let anyone else call me that. Just like the horror films, tree house and rewards, that belongs to us.

Nineteen

JACE

I missed Nate's graduation today. I wanted to see him walk across that stage. I thought this would finally be the week I'd go back home but when mom told me about his boyfriend being there, I changed my mind. He's finally moved on. I made my mom believe I did too, right before he started seeing him by telling her some bullshit lie about me dating some girl who lives up the road. Lindsey is real and has taken a liking to me, but I've never returned her feelings. We never dated and I've told her many times that I was in love with someone else.

"Does she know?" She asked, fluttering her blonde lashes at me.

I told her she was a 'he' and he did. At least I hope he still did. She asked me if he felt the same after giving me a doe eyed stare and I didn't know how to answer her. He did once. But I guess that love has now been given to someone else. Did I expect him to wait forever? Did I expect him to remain lonely and longing like me? This was and is my choice. Me staying away was never his so only I deserve to suffer for it. Looks like only I will too.

I kick the dirt with my boot, heading out to the pond. With my fishing pole in hand, I look ahead, shielding the sun from my eyes. It was beautiful out here. I truly had it made being able to fish whenever I wanted and watch the sun go down from the water. I'd gladly give it all up to hold him again. To tell him I love him and know for sure if he still feels the same. To hear him say that the man he's seeing was only temporary. Such a selfish thought. My head is full of them when it comes to him and that's one of the many reasons' he's better off. Moving way past the trees, I stop in front of the partially drugged man on the ground and untie his ropes. Leaning down further, I smile at him while he mutters something under his breath, and I shove a fishhook through his bottom lip. He screeches and shakes his head, unable to lift his hands very far. I don't want to think about why I brought him out here again and what he did. It's too vile and made my stomach churn when I first heard about it on the news. I don't need to either. I only need to punish him for breaking the rules. For breaking my rules.

"Let's go fishing, shall we. The water's nice around this time."

He kicks and screams as I drag him toward the water. I shove him forward, causing him to make a giant splash. I laugh, using the line to pull him up and out of the water, the hook creating a larger hole in his skin. And this right here is another reason Nate is better off.

Twenty

NATE

"Oh, come on, just close your eyes for a few minutes," my boyfriend Glen says, taking my hand.

"But what if I accidentally walk off the deck and straight into the lake?"

He laughs, kissing my ear. "I won't let you."

"But—"

"Just do this for me, please."

I blow out a long sigh, slumping my arms in defeat. "Fine. I just don't understand what you have to show me out here that I haven't already seen."

"You'll see soon enough," he says, smiling.

"Not if you're making me close my eyes," I grind out, and that earns me another laugh from him.

I take one more look around us before shutting my eyes and letting Glen slowly pull me forward, my shoes occasionally clipping onto the wood with uncertainty.

"Are you keeping them closed?"

"Yes," I say, sounding impatient and annoyed.

"No peeking, you hear?"

"Alright, alright." I let out a soft grunt and he doesn't say anything for a long time, my chest fluttering in anticipation. Why are we out here on such a cold day? What could he possibly show me out here that I haven't seen before, and why is he so damn quiet suddenly?

The boards wobble under my feet and I wipe my sweaty palm on my pants, feeling him tug at my other hand slightly as something hits the deck with a soft thud.

Oh no. Please tell me this isn't what I think it is? It can't be. I have to be getting it wrong. My heart rate picks up, breaths shallowing as he clears his throat.

No. No. No. It's happening. It's actually happening. It was only a matter of time, right? I've been with the guy for three years, what did I expect? For him to want to play unserious boyfriend forever?

He's known where my heart lies this whole time—I've made sure of it. He says he doesn't care when I know he does, but I think he's holding on to hope like I still am, only we're doing it with different people in mind.

I thought if I dated others, making it look like I've moved on, Jace would finally come back, and my mom wouldn't hesitate so much whenever she tried to invite him over for the holidays. But neither has happened. Jace is still there and I'm still here, wishing the man in front of me was someone else.

A knot forms in my throat when a kiss is pressed to my knuckles. "You can open your eyes now," Glen says, sounding more nervous than I feel.

When my lids slowly peel back, Glen is on one knee, holding a black velvet box in his hands. All the air leaves my lungs. I hold on to the railing to remain steady on my feet, my heart racing a million miles a minute against my pressing hand. I already know the answer to his question before he asks it. No doubt in my mind it's the right one either. On the other hand, when I so much as entertain the idea of saying yes, all dread seeps in tenfold.

"Nate. I never thought I could fall so quickly for someone until I met you. I can't imagine going on without you forever at my side." He takes a breath, his smile shaking. "Will you make me the happiest man alive and be my husband?" I place my hand on top of the box, shutting it as he attempts to pop it open.

"I . . ." I rub a hand roughly over my face, closing my mouth before opening it again. "I could never love you the way you want me to."

"You don't know that." His eyes are begging and I feel like shit for putting him in this position. This started as a fling. Something to pass the time and fill a temporary void—nothing serious. I told him over and over. Still, he broke the rules and fell for me anyway. He isn't the only one who fell for the wrong person. I recognize the desperation and heartache in his eyes. Seven years ago I saw the same emotion pouring from my reflection in a bathroom mirror. I hated myself that day, and I hate myself now too.

I cup his face, leaning down. "Yes I do. My heart belongs to another and always will, whether he's with me or not. I'll never fully be yours or anyone else's."

"You'll see with time, anything is possible. He's gone and I'm here. Please let me stay." His words shake. He doesn't know who "he" is, only about there being someone before him.

I swallow back the emotion in my throat and shake my head. When I try to pull away, he holds onto me, keeping me in place. "At least think about it."

"It won't do either of us any good. If I say yes to you, I'll only hurt you in the end. He could walk through that door after we make promises to each other and I'll probably still run into his arms. Is that what you want? You shouldn't settle for anything less than you deserve."

"And neither should you." He squeezes my fingers, his intense gaze holding mine, but not for the reason he wants it to.

"He's been gone for how long now? What makes you think he's coming back? When was the last time you heard from him?"

"Seven years," I whisper. But I swear he left a little bit of him behind everywhere I go. It's what my heart wants to believe.

"How about instead of waiting for something that might never happen, you take a chance with me and let me give you what you need now."

"And what's that?"

"Love. Devotion. To be here every time you need someone to lean on. He can't give you that and I can. Let me. We'll worry about the what-ifs later."

"You don't know what you're asking."

"I'm asking for you. I just want you. Exactly as you are."

My chest aches with each inhale and exhale. I think over his words before saying, "Okay. But what I said before is all still true. I'll marry you as long as you can live with the fact that someone else will always be my first choice."

He gets to his feet, letting go of my hand only long enough to open the box and slip the ring on my finger. "We'll see about that."

I want to say I hope he's right, but even if losing feelings and forgetting about Jace would make my life easier, I don't want to ever feel less for him than I do now. It wouldn't feel right to. He was meant to be mine and I was meant to be his. I just need him to find his way back to me.

I don't stop him from opening the box again, and hold out my hand so he can slip the gorgeous simple silver band with a small diamond heart in the center on my finger. I'm not a materialistic person, or huge on wearing jewelry, but I am very sentimental. I love having proof of special moments, and Glen really wants to make sure I hang on to all the ones he feels we share.

His eyes light up and he kisses my hand again, getting back up to his feet to press his lips to mine. I smile against his mouth and it's not forced. I do feel a little happiness, because he is a good guy, and even though I don't feel like I deserve so much understanding from him, he gives it to me anyway. He might be right and Jace may never come back. If I really had to spend the rest of my life with someone else, Glen would be the best choice.

I do care for him, and though the love I feel may not be the same as what I have for Jace, it's still there. And who knows, maybe over time I can really be what he needs me to be. Maybe Jace can really feel like nothing but a brother to me someday, and Glen can be my new everything. Just maybe.

Glen kisses me again and whistles loudly, signaling for others to join us from a distance. My eyes widen when my parents rush forward to congratulate us. I stand frozen at the loud squeals from our close friends and other family. How close were they when I shared my uncertainty with him? Nothing about their expressions gives away that they heard anything I said, and he did have to make a noise to alert them to come out. He had it all planned out this way. He knew I'd have my doubts and worries.

But I don't know if he did this for me or him? Who did he try to save from embarrassment? I'd never have to question any of this with Jace. He was always thinking about others before himself.

"Oh, honey. I'm so happy for you both." My mom embraces me in a hug while my dad taps me on the shoulder. My bio mom of course is nowhere to be seen, but I'm used to her being absent by now. She had an excuse for not showing up to my high-school and college graduation, so I'm sure she'd come up with some other blatant lie this time too. I don't need her here anyway. I don't need her at all. The person I truly want to see isn't here, and I can't expect him to be either.

"I tried to invite your brother but he's a hard guy to reach," Glen whispers in my ear, resting a hand at the hilt of my back.

I swallow the dryness in my throat, stomach tightening. Does that mean he never answered? He knows my brother and I are estranged, but he also knows he's an important person in my life. I guess he didn't want to leave him out even if he knew there was no chance of him coming.

"Yeah, he's not a huge fan of phones."

"Yeah, I've noticed. Email definitely worked better. Your mom gave me his address when I asked, and he said he'd try to make it." He stares at me with a proud look in his eyes.

All I can do is stand here tongue tied, losing all ability to speak and think. Right when I feel I'm ready to move again, a tall, slender figure stands between all the smiling faces, his face neutral and eyes distant. My heart rattles in my chest, breaths sticking to the back of my throat. He's here. He actually came. Why now?

His hair is longer, the bottom half of his face covered in dark facial hair, but he still looks like the Jace I remember. Only older and more serious. He's wearing dark jeans and his old hoodie, and he gives me a short nod.

"Is that him?" Glen's mouth brushes over my ear, eyes locked on the man I'm still expecting to disappear at any given moment.

"Yes," I answer, fully unsure of who he means. The answer applies either way, but he doesn't know that.

"Jace," my mom shouts. "Is that really you?"

"Well look who finally emerged from the farm," my dad says, voice sounding humorous, and Glen relaxes beside me, kissing my cheek.

"Hey, Dad. I see you decided to grow that mustache out after all. Looks like you belong where I live more than I do now."

Mom lets out a short laugh, her face unreadable. After all this time she should be happy he's here. He's her son after all. I wonder if she thinks he came here to mess this up for me. It seemed to be her thinking all those years ago.

"I don't think he means to do it," she said to me. "I think his mind just operates differently than ours. After what he's been through."

I bite the inside of my cheeks, the taste of copper hitting my tongue. Her words stung my ears, leaving behind a poisonous taste in my mouth.

"It's good to see you, son," Dad says, wrapping Jace in a tight hug. I stay where I am, still in disbelief. I'm scared that if I get too close he'll vanish the way he does when I wake up from my dreams.

"Hey, little brother," he says so damn casually as if we've spoken only recently, flicking his eyes down to me. My height hasn't caught up to his yet. He towers over me more now than he did then. He looks good. Too damn good. But what did I expect? This is Jace we're talking about. The man who always managed to take my breath away every time he looked my way.

"Hey," I say, not recognizing my own voice.

"Congratulations. This must be the lucky fella." His eyes bounce between mine and Glen's.

"Yeah. This is Glen. Glen this is—"

"The infamous Jace. I know. Nice to finally meet you. This one talks about you all the time and all the adventures you've been on together."

Jace cocks his head. "Does he now? Hopefully he hasn't told you anything too embarrassing." His lips form into a wavering smile.

"Nah, not at all. Well, maybe a little. But what brother doesn't." Glen laughs, stepping forward. "I hope you'll be joining us for dinner and the celebratory drinks afterward."

Jace sucks his teeth, eyes back on me. "Sounds like a fun time."

"You can ride with us, hun," Mom says, smiling between us.

"Or he can come with us. We have plenty of room. I'm sure Nate would like to spend more time with his brother."

My mom's brows lift, forehead wrinkling. "Well, it's completely up to you." She lays a hand on Jace's arm, her eyes passing a message only the two of them can understand.

He nods. "Yeah, sure. It'll give me time to size you up a little, make sure you're right for Nate. You know, like big brothers should do."

"Great. So it's been decided then."

I open my mouth to argue, closing it when Glen guides Jace to his SUV. I follow them, waving everyone else off, and my stomach folds in on itself when Jace sits up front with Glen. Feeling uneasy about this whole situation, I hop in the back, listening carefully as they talk about what Jace has been up to on the farm. How many animals he has and if he plans on coming back home to Texas anytime soon.

"No plans as of yet." He looks back at me and then at Glen. "My uncle isn't doing too well health wise and has mentioned wanting me to take over the farm. He thinks I'm the perfect man for the job and I really don't feel like there's anything else out there for me." Uncle Judd had a heart attack after being hit in the chest by one of his horses a year ago and hasn't been the same since, so I can understand my aunt wanting him to retire sooner than planned. He's also sixteen years older than my dad and has never cared much for managing his diabetes.

"Really?" I say, not realizing the words actually came out until Jace is watching me again.

"Yeah . . . I like the quiet, simple life out there, and it's a free feeling working out in the open. You know how much I've always enjoyed the outdoors."

"Yeah, I do." I remember well how full of life he looked whenever he was standing under the bright sunlight or breathing in the fall air, spinning around in flying leaves. "It was hard to get your ass inside some days."

He scoffs. "Right. As if you cared to be indoors yourself. You loved the water parks, drive-ins, and festivals."

"You're right, I did. None of that feels the same anymore." Not without you.

"Yeah. Things do seem different here." He shifts in his seat, looking ahead.

"I wouldn't know," Glen adds, reminding us both of his presence. "I didn't grow up here like you two. College brought me here and well, Nate kept me here." He shoots me a quick smile before turning onto the road the restaurant's on.

Jace asks the questions next, wanting to know how we met and how long we've been together. Guilt settles in my gut when Glen is way too excited to answer, smiling as he talks about the party he first saw me at and how he couldn't take his eyes off me.

I look at Jace, wishing I could see his face and know what he's thinking. Is he truly happy for me or is he as jealous as I would be if our roles were reversed? I was more relieved than I should be when he showed up here alone. Not like it matters. Not like he wants me like that anymore.

Doesn't mean I can't want him to anyway. I tried to move on. I'm still trying. I'm sitting in the back seat of my new fiancé's car, twisting my engagement ring on my finger, wishing I could stop wanting to be alone with the wrong person. Wishing I could stop wanting him to look at me the way he used to and beg me not to go for it.

Twenty-One

JACE

When I first saw the email, I wanted to delete it and pretend it never existed. But then I thought about how many of the wrong guys he'd fallen for in the past and how I had to make sure this guy was what he truly needed. That this guy really deserved him and was worthy. I knew seeing him would be hard but I wasn't prepared for how much.

He keeps looking at me with confused and angry eyes. They're hard to look away from. He's hard to look away from. Missing him is one of the fucking reasons, and the other being what a gorgeous man he's grown into. More breathtaking than ever with honey-colored hair and luscious pink lips. He keeps licking and biting them, shifting from side to side as we wait to be seated at a table.

Mom and Dad are right behind us when a waitress grabs our menus and leads us to a back corner. Nate sits by the window and Glen sits across from him, reaching for his hand while telling me how often they've been here together. As if I give a shit about Nate being anywhere with anyone else but me. As if I care to hear this guy's voice more than I was already forced to in the car.

I bite my tongue to stop myself from telling him all the places I've been too. The parts of Nate I got to visit before him or anyone else.

He seems nice enough. Good looking with a decent paying job and genuine love for my brother. All his constant random touches and smiles tell me how much he adores him. Probably for all the same reasons I did, and still do. As I circle around the table to take the seat next to Nate, my mom squeezes between us, and my dad has a confused look on his face when she does. I shake it off and walk back around, lowering myself next to Glen.

My dad asks me about what I've been up to, and all focus is on me for the next thirty minutes as more questions are thrown my way. My mom keeps watching me as if waiting for me to jump across the table and attack Nate like some predator on Animal Planet. The trust will never be there no matter what I do. I've stayed away all this time, and came back to show how supportive of this new relationship I am. What more does she want?

I'm pretending not to care, hiding my jealousy and primal urges. Holding back the need to show Nate who he should be marrying instead. And it's fucking painful. I want to crawl out of my damn skin the tighter it feels around my bones. I'm doing all this for her and him—because it's what's right. Only, I'm not getting the same satisfaction from it as I did when I dragged a fucking serial rapist by his dick with my tractor yesterday.

Hearing his screams and his begging for me to stop felt good, but this is fucking torture. This is where I'm still that bad person. Unable to free him from my heart and to stop thinking all the wrong thoughts when he's near.

I want to snatch his hand away from Glen and hold it in mine again. I want to kiss his soft fingers and feel them all over my body. I want all the things I need to forget about wanting. He's marrying someone else, and he'll be much happier with him than he ever was with me.

Maybe he doesn't look as excited as a newly engaged man should, but I'm sure that has to do with my presence. The shock on his face hasn't fully faded and he hasn't said much this whole time. It's almost as if he's forgotten how to act around me. Or is the new him truly this quiet and easily agreeable.

Glen orders for both of them, food Nate has never cared for before. He asks the waitress to refill Nate's cup when it's half empty. His "thank you" is almost too quiet and his smiles come off uneasy. Yeah, I should have stayed gone. If I knew I'd cause him this much distress and discomfort while being here, I would never have shown.

The Nate sitting a few seats away from me is unrecognizable, moving like a robot with the usual bright light he once held in his eyes almost nonexistent. Am I the only one who notices the difference? You would think so by the way everyone is carrying on normally, laughing and cracking jokes.

"Are you staying with me and Dad?" Mom asks, tucking a loose strand of hair behind her ear.

"I actually got a hotel. I didn't want to put you guys out."

"Why would you do that when you still have a perfectly good room at the house?" My dad dabs his mouth with a napkin, raising a brow. "You too cool to stay with your mom and dad now?"

Mom waves him off. "Oh hun, you know you can't force him. If he wants to stay somewhere else, he can. He knows our door is always open if he changes his mind." Her smile tightens.

"Why not stay with Nate?" Glen suggests. "He has a three-bedroom house with plenty of room. I know how much he complains about being in that big house by himself all the time."

Nate's eyes widen, shoulders lifting and face tensing.

My stomach twists at his response. Yeah, he's nothing like the person I remember. He'd be the first to talk me into staying over and having late-night movie nights. "Oh, I wouldn't want to impose. It's y'alls engagement night after all. I'd think you'd want your privacy."

One of Glen's shoulders lift and he casually reaches for his iced water. "You wouldn't be. If anything you'd be doing me a favor, keeping this one company when I can't. Sadly I have a flight at five a.m. and need to leave for the airport at three. Business meeting out of town."

"You didn't tell me," Nate says, sitting up higher in his chair. "How long will you be gone?"

Glen leans back in his chair, lifting his cup to his parting lips. "I thought I did yesterday? Besides, it's only a couple of days, cutie. You'll be so busy catching up with your brother and work you'll hardly notice I'm gone."

"I actually have to head out in the morning too," I blurt. "I'm not sure the new farm hand can handle three days without me."

"But you just got here," Nate says unexpectedly.

Tongue tied, I gulp down some of my tea and nod. "Yeah, I know, and I probably shouldn't have left with all the work needing to be done, but I didn't want to miss another important moment in my brother's life."

"That's sweet. I'm sure Nate appreciates any time you're willing to spare, even though I think it'd make him really happy to get to see more of you. I'm glad we had the chance to finally meet." Glen smiles, setting his glass down.

"Yeah, me too." I force a smile, not sure I believe my own words.

The food comes and we all eat, Nate saying even less than before. Thankfully, the remainder of the questions aren't all pointed toward me and are more for Glen. Mom is so interested in this guy, beaming at him every time he opens his mouth. He's very charming, no doubt. The more perfect he comes off, the more wary I get.

My dad was the same around other people. Strangers saw him as this family man who was in good standing with his community. He volunteered, donated to charities, and to everyone but me he was the perfect parent who wanted the best for his son. His selfish ways were hidden behind a big fake smile and all the right words.

I think I will stay for the rest of the week after all. It'll give me more time to dig up more on this guy and see what Nate's like when he's gone. Will he be the old version of himself I've come to know, or will he be this other person who only looks like Nate?

Is he putting on an act too? Or is this what happiness looks like on him now that we're older? I'm not sure if I'm relieved or saddened by how empty his eyes look when they're on Glen. I don't see the same love there I see in his fiancé's. Does he feel like he needs to hide it all from me? Is this all for my benefit?

I expect his smiles to be more believable when we reach the bar and Glen is sliding a drink into his hand, but they're as plastic as they were at the restaurant, never fully reaching his eyes. Glen just keeps kissing him and holding his hand without noticing. Without any kind of alarm. He's either not paying enough attention or this is the only version of my brother he's ever known.

If that's the case, I'm both sad and sorry for him. For anyone who hasn't experienced all the sides I have. I'm also greedy and hoping I'm right. That he doesn't know all there is to know about the wonderful man he keeps trying to pull into his lap while slurring sweet, sappy words. That he didn't get the parts of him only I had the pleasure of having. That he doesn't get to have what's only meant to be mine.

Except he isn't mine anymore, and the ring on his finger is proof of that. Someone else holding and touching him is proof of that.

My heart plummets as the realization dawns on me. He really isn't mine anymore. Seeing it is harder than hearing the words. It's more real. More crushing. Each breath is more painful the longer I watch them. Maybe Nate isn't smiling with him the way he did with me, and maybe he doesn't get everything I did, but he gets him. He gets him whenever he wants and wherever he wants. They don't have to shield their love from the public and feel shameful about it in front of others.

And I know it sounds stupid and irrational, but I can't help but feel like Glen is doing it to rub it in my face. To prove some point. That I might have had the best of him but I have nothing now.

Finding it harder to breathe when Nate turns into Glen, laughing against his lips, I shove my way through a group of people and rush outside. As soon as the fresh, warm air hits my face, I close my eyes and breathe more of it in. Lifting my face toward the sky, I tug at my hair and bite back the scream threatening to escape my lips.

I have nothing. Absolutely nothing. All the success, money, peaceful life doesn't matter if I don't have him. None of it ever will. Is that the real reason I came here? So I could stop running from the truth? So I could stop trying to play make believe like he is tonight?

When I turn around, my pulse pounds loudly in my ears. Nate stands in front of me, chest rising and falling heavily. "After all this time, why come back now? After all this time of ignoring me and leaving me behind, why now?"

His words pierce my heart. "I . . . I wanted to make sure you were happy."

"And then what?" His voice strains. "Then fucking what?"

"I . . . I don't know." I tug at my hair. "I don't know."

"You thought it would free you of your guilt? Make you feel better about being gone? To know that I found more happiness because of it? To see proof of me being better off? Well I didn't and I'm not. Is that what you wanted to hear?" Tears spring to his eyes and he backs away when I try to reach for him.

"Why did you come back, Jace? Why?"

The back door opens and Glen appears, eyes lifting in our direction. "Oh, there you two are. Everything okay?"

Nate rubs his eyes and turns around, putting on that faulty smile again. "Yeah. Just got a little stuffy in there is all, and I think my allergies are acting up again."

Glen moves closer to us with worry in his expression. "Let's get you home then. I need to get some rest anyway. Your parents said they're heading out too. You should go say bye to them."

"Yeah. I'll go do that." He looks back at me. "You coming?"

"Yeah." I follow him back into the club, Glen patting my shoulder as I pass him. My parents are already walking to the exit, my dad picking up his steps when he sees us.

"Y'all weren't trying to sneak out without us, were you?" my dad says.

"Of course not," Nate exclaims. "We just needed some fresh air."

"Good, because we were hoping you liked us more than that," my dad chimes, Mom chuckling beside him.

"Only a little bit more," I chirp and everyone laughs, Nate's smile dying too quickly. Seeing it briefly makes me need to see more—so much more. I'm entering dangerous territory and I know I'll do anything for more of those smiles if I stay too long. And the short time it takes to hug him goodbye at Glen's car after they drop me off is way too damn long.

Twenty-Two

NATE

I thought I could do it—get through a car ride, dinner, and a few drinks with him. I thought I could make it through three days of him visiting, but then he wraps those familiar warm arms around me, brushing his lips against my ear, and I nearly lose all composure.

When he pulls away to walk to his car, it takes so much restraint not to follow him and pull his body into mine again. He smelled so damn good too. Exactly how I remembered. Fresh grass and jasmine. I wanted to bury my nose in him, drowning in the scent until I was unable to smell anything else ever again.

"Goodnight, little brother," he says, with one side of his lips lifting. "Maybe I'll see you at Mom Dad's tomorrow for dinner."

"Maybe," I say back, both thankful and a little hurt that he'd turned down Glen's offer to crash at my place. I'd stopped myself from shooting him a glare when he made the suggestion. He thought he was helping. Glen always thinks he's helping by pushing me to my limits to prevent me from missing out on opportunities.

This is one he'd certainly want me to miss out on, though, and he doesn't even know it yet. I hope he never finds out either. Jace being here increases those chances, so if he plans to walk away and never come back again, he might as well leave now. Or is he here as some test to see which of us was really the problem all this time? Which one is the weakest and struggles with crossing boundaries more? To prove how much he got in my way by being here?

He's already losing if that's the case, because I'm not the one who stayed away. I'm not the one who gave up on us. I was never influenced to do anything I didn't want to do. Does he really think being engaged will erase what my heart's been carrying for him all these years? Not a day has gone by where I haven't messaged him to tell him I was thinking about him. Not one single day. He didn't ever answer, but I hoped he at least read everything I sent him, and I hope that's the real reason he's here.

"Family is important," Glen says as he drops me off in front of my house, brushing soft lips over my chin. "And I can tell how much you missed him."

Could he really?

I hated him for leaving, but I hate him even more coming back. For reminding me of what I've lost. Of what he's been keeping from us because of other people's opinions. He let them keep us apart. He didn't bother to ask me if it's what I needed, he just assumed it was. I only needed him. Three more days and he'll be gone again. He'll be back at the farm and I'll be planning my wedding. Will he show up to the ceremony? Will he ask to dance with me at the reception?

After kissing Glen back, I hurry inside. I watch from the window as he drives away and reach for my phone. No new messages or calls. Why would there be? Pretty much everyone I know was out with us tonight. I guess

I thought maybe after seeing me in person after all this time, Jace would finally answer my messages.

Tapping the screen, I search for his name. I write a message and delete it before writing another. After continuous back and forth, I finally hit send.

Me: Why are you really here?

My heart jumps when dots dance across the screen, and then they disappear leaving behind a sinking sensation in my stomach. I keep checking my phone the rest of the night—before showering, after dressing in comfortable clothes, and while I'm lounging on the couch watching reruns of *Reba*.

I want to know why he's really here. I'm not buying his reasons. If he'd truly cared about me being happy he would have joined me at university like he was supposed to. He would have shown up at the apartment I set up for us, helping me choose better curtains after telling me how awful my first choice was. We'd have laughed and kissed. He'd have tucked hair behind my ear and tugged me closer to him, right before our bodies stayed locked together for hours as we lay naked under the covers.

Fuck, I miss him. My heart pains and I rest my head against the suede cushion, blowing out a loud sigh. I saw him today and still miss him. He wasn't necessarily cold, but distant. Proof he hasn't found his way back to me yet. Will he ever? He said he'll be going to dinner tomorrow. Since Glen won't be there, will he be more like he used to be? At least the brother side of him, or my best friend who'd cover my eyes during scary scenes? The guy who'd order different food than me so we could eat off each other's plates? Would he buy packs of Starbursts so he could purposely save me all the orange ones?

Yeah, I miss him. I really, really do. And at this point I'll take what he gives me if it means I get to have him in my life somehow. In some fucking way. His short answers and small talk are better than the silence that's stood between us for too long. Occasional dinners during special occasions will at least lead to us sitting at the same table again, if only once every few years. They aren't enough, though. I can try to make them be all I want, but the truth will always remain—I really can't do this, and if he leaves again he might truly destroy me this time. My heart will be too broken for me to move forward with the man who actually fought to keep me.

I really would be better off if Jace hadn't come back at all.

Twenty-Three

JACE

I kept going back to his message all night long, beginning to write some bullshit answers several times, and hitting delete before finishing each one. I'm hiding from the truth myself. I can give him all the answers I've told myself but I'll be leaving out the main reason every time.

I'm here because I want his perfect boyfriend to be more wrong for him than I am. It's fucked up. This doesn't mean I don't want the best for him, because I do. He deserves everything good in the world but I can't stop wanting to be the one to give it to him. But what if everyone else is right and I really can't? What if Prince Charming really is the better option?

Then I'll be on my way, and go back to keeping my distance. He hasn't stopped sending me messages, and I hadn't been able to stop myself from unblocking him to confirm whether he had. I also missed those "I need you" messages too much. Those words are being said less and less these days, though.

Is it because he's saying them to someone else now? Is Glen truly all he needs? Why did he look so lost and sad then? Why did the love between them only appear to be one-sided? Did me being so close make him feel bad for showing his true feelings for Glen?

When I arrive at my parents' house, the sun has gone from hot to boiling on my exposed skin. Everything is exactly how I remember. Blue flowers appear from the bushes under the windows, and a brown wooden rocking chair sits on the faded-blue porch with a pillow held up against the armrest, reading "Home Sweet Home." The pink stone path leading to the house holds a few cracks and wear, and I pick up my strides when the front door opens.

The pillow's words have never felt more true when I gaze into a pair of stunned blue eyes I could get lost in for days.

"What are you doing here?" Nate straightens his neck, holding on tightly to the gold door knob as if needing it to help him stay up right.

"I told you I was coming for dinner," I say, inching closer and staring down at his unmoving hand blocking me from entering the house and escaping the thickening heat.

"Yes, but dinner isn't for another few hours. You're really early."

"And so are you." I smile smugly. "What can I say? I hate hotel rooms and wanted to see if my old room really was still the same."

"It is," he snaps, anger vibrating through his words. I don't blame him. I told him I'd always be here for him but I haven't been in a long time. Watching from a distance wasn't good enough, and he's letting me know that with his short responses and daggering stares.

"You going to let me see for myself, or what?" My lips curl and he nods, stepping back.

"Be my guest. Mom and Dad won't be home from work for a while. I only had one virtual appointment today since the second person canceled on me."

"Virtual appointment? Does that mean you went on to being a therapist after all?"

"Yes. Some of us stay true to our words." He slams the door shut behind me, shaking the pictures on the walls. None of them have me in them and I feel like I've intruded on the wrong family. Nate is smiling with Glen in one and fishing with Dad in another.

The perfect, do-good fiancé somehow earned his place in those frames over me. Although I did typically shy away from photos unless Nate was the cameraman. As I'm about to question my true place in this house, that's when I spot it. On the fireplace mantle rests a photo of me and Nate on graduation day, right next to one of us dressed for prom. I smile, running my fingers over the frame and tracing the happiness displayed on both our faces.

"I thought you wanted to see your room?"

I turn around, tilting my head, and ignore the itch in my fingers to reach out and touch him. "Yeah, but I figured I'd take a trip down memory lane first and see what other important memories Dad's captured while I was gone."

"You walked past my college graduation photo." I think back to the photo of him and Glen, remembering the cap and gown he was sporting. Of course Mr. Perfect was there for one of the most important days of his life. Why does he act like he needed me there too? He replaced me and the evidence is everywhere. How long did he wait to truly move on?

I know he hung out with other guys way after I left, telling me all about where he went and sharing embarrassing moments. He also mentioned how unsatisfied he was each time and I'm waiting for him to do it again with Glen. Why was he the lucky one who got to stay and become more? And did he make Nate squirm and moan the way I did whenever I kissed his sensitive spots?

"I saw it. You and Glen really are the perfect couple."

"Is that really what you think?" He scrutinizes me with his eyes.

"Yes, but even in things that are perfect, hidden flaws lie ready to be unburied."

"Is that why you're here? To try and unbury them? You're still trying to save me from the world, aren't you?" he shouts. "Well, I don't need you to. You came to congratulate me and now you can return to your farm."

"And I will once my visit is over."

"I waited for you." His voice shakes. "I waited and waited. Did you even care at all?"

My stomach shifts, his sadness spreading across my chest like a thousand knives. "Do you really want me to answer that question?"

"Yes. Why did you stay away for so long? Why did you break your promises?"

"I didn't want to. It was better that I did, though. Look how well you're doing. You have everything you could ever want."

"But I don't have you." His words cut deep into my heart, slicing it right in half.

"You don't need me. Especially when you have him now. He seems good for you."

He looks down at his shuffling feet. "He is. Too good. He deserves more than I can give him. Someone who's not already hopelessly in love with someone else." He peers back up at me, holding my stare.

"Nate."

"If you plan to leave again, why not get it over with? Why drag it on and leave more memories behind for me to sulk in?" His eyes water, and he slaps my hand away the way he did yesterday when I tried to offer him some comfort by running my fingers over his skin. Would I have stopped there, though? I'm not sure I would have been able to. Not with the way he tucked his bottom lip between his teeth and how the curling tips of his hair begged my fingers to tug on them.

"I'm not leaving because I want to. I'm leaving because—"

"Save me the bullshit." He lifts a shaky hand between us. "I don't want to hear how you're doing this for me. How you're trying to do the right thing. Because you and I . . ." He points between us, jabbing me in the chest. "Were never wrong. We weren't."

"Mom wouldn't agree. Most people wouldn't. Glen wouldn't either."

He laughs mockingly, shaking his head. "Why do you keep bringing him up in this?"

"Because he's your fiancé, and if he knew about us he would never have written me that email. He would never have suggested I stay with you so we could reconnect."

"He comforted me on my worst days, you know. He forced me back into the world on days I wanted to shut it all away." His voice grew smaller and I wanted nothing more than to take him in my arms. "Do you plan on showing up for the wedding too? Or are you going to disappear for another seven years?"

"I don't know yet." He inches closer, the air growing thin between us and the smell of his shampoo clouding my better judgement. He's right, if I'm going to leave anyway, I might as well get it over with. Which is so damn hard to do when everything in me is screaming to stay. When his needy stares are begging me to stay. He says we were never wrong, and I want to believe that more than anything. But I can't stop seeing the disappointment in my mom's eyes. I can't stop seeing the worry and blame she held for me at dinner last night. I'm not sure I'll be able to erase it from my memory if she does it again tonight either. And I don't think I could handle him looking at me the same way when he discovers how I've been quieting my nightmares.

"I'm still waiting for you, Jace," he whispers against my lips. "I don't know how to stop."

"I'm right here."

"No you aren't. Not in the way you should be." He lets out a breath, rubbing the back of his head. "You should go do what you said you came here to do. Mom really did keep your room exactly the same."

"You go in there often or something?" I say, tugging at his arm when he tries to walk away.

"I . . ." He nibbles on his bottom lip, unable to meet my eyes. "Yeah. Every time I come here."

My heart flutters and I run my fingers through his hair, not being stopped this time. I tug at the soft strands and he tilts his head back, releasing a soft moan.

"I don't want to leave you. I've never wanted to leave you. But you deserve so much more than me. Someone who's not as flawed and broken."

His eyes flash open and he holds on to my wrist. "The man I'm looking at now is none of those things."

I swallow the lump in my throat, wishing what he said was true. The nightmares prove otherwise. So do everyone's wary eyes every time I enter a room full of familiar faces in this town. Why won't he see what he's supposed to see? If he did, leaving him again would be a lot easier. The pull between us is stronger than ever. An invisible string connects us, immediately synching back together no matter how many times I cut at it.

A loud beep sounds outside and we both drop our hands, breaking away from each other like the old days. Some things really don't change, do they?

The front door snicks open and Dad appears, smiling. "Jace. You really came. Mom is going to be really happy to have both her boys in the house at the same time again."

Is she? Doubt nudges its ugly head into my gut. "Yeah, I'm here and will be for the next three days. I let everyone know I'll be back by Monday. They all ensured they could survive without me for a little while."

"And I'm sure they can." My dad squeezes my arm. "It's really good to have you back, son. Hopefully these visits will become a habit."

"They just might," I say with way too much hope in my voice. Nate flashes me a look before turning away to walk toward the kitchen.

"I'm gonna get me a drink. Anyone want anything?"

"I'll join you." I jump forward, earning a wide-eyed expression from him.

"I'm okay," Dad says, setting down his briefcase. "I'm going to be in my office for the next hour grading papers. If you boys need anything, feel free to come knocking."

Dad disappears down the short hall and I follow Nate into the kitchen. Opening the fridge, he grabs himself a bottle of water and hands me a Coke.

I hold the cold can in my hand, tilting my head.

"What? I was curious to see if you still drank them."

"On occasion." I pop the top, taking a long sip. "I'm more of a sweet-tea guy these days."

"What else has changed?" He closes the fridge, turning fully my way.

"Not too much." Not anything that matters. My heart continues to beat only for him. My skin yearns for him to press against it and I haven't stopped searching out his body in my sleep.

"Something tells me that isn't true. Are you seeing anyone out there?"

"Why? Would you be jealous if I was?" I say with a little humor etched in my voice.

He scoffs. "Hardly." His eyes narrow in on me. "Are you jealous of Glen?"

"Hardly," I say back, wearing a shit-eating grin.

His face hardens and he steps back. "You ever going to go see that room of yours?"

"Sure. After you show me yours. I want to see if yours is the same too."

"You don't need to see mine." He quickly turns away from me, leaning against the counter and pretending to look out the window.

"Maybe not, but will you show me anyway?"

"Are you going to want a tour of the bathroom next?" he asks with sarcasm laced in his tone as he turns his head slightly.

"Maybe. Depends on whether Mom ended up getting that wallpaper she always talked about."

A laugh rushes out of him and the light, welcoming sound lasts longer than it did yesterday. The perfect melody in my ears. I'm glad to know he hasn't lost that part of him because of me.

"Let's get this little tour of yours over with then." He walks back into the living room and I follow, nearly running into him several times as we head up the stairs.

Tan carpet has replaced the wooden floor on each step we walk up, leading all the way to our rooms. New decor is scattered across the walls and there's a plant in the corner I don't recognize. Nate leads us into his room first, and the only thing that's changed are the curtains. Hanging above his bed and covering his window is the same set he texted me a picture of when he was still in college. They're even tackier in person, managing to drag another smile from me. As awful as they are, they're perfect.

I run my hands along the too-busy pattern, sparks bouncing between us when his fingers touch a spot so close to mine our skin brushes together.

"I brought them here after I moved out of the apartment. I thought they belonged here. Where we were last together."

A flutter settles in my stomach and I trace above his wedding band. "They're perfect."

His lips twitch in the corners and he leaves his hand where it is, allowing me to drag my fingers along the pulse point of his wrist. I've kissed him there plenty of times before, his skin the perfect mixture of salty and sweet on my tongue.

"You wouldn't have changed them if you'd come home?"

"I'm not sure what I'd have done then, but I know I wouldn't change them now. I actually think they'd look great in my office."

"You have an office?"

"Kinda." I shrug. "The closest thing to one. It's in the old barn. Uncle Judd had no use for it anymore so I turned it into my own space. I even sleep in there sometimes, on a cheap futon. I like being close to the animals. Their sounds might keep others up at night but I find them soothing."

"I could see that. I mean, they did invent frog machines for a reason," he teases, giving me more of his arm to caress, to mark up with my skin.

"I need to stop," I say, sliding my fingers under the sleeve of his shirt, touching slightly above his nipple.

His body quivers, breaths short and fast. "You should."

"I need you to stop me," I say between pants, tracing around his areola.

"I've never been good at it before. What makes you think I would be now?" His bright blue eyes darken, lips parting as he sucks in a breath from me tugging at the hard nub.

"And I've never been able to resist you."

"I never asked you to," he says between soft moans, writhing against my hip. His cock digs into my inner thigh as I turn more into him and brush my lips along his collar bone, licking a stripe into his skin.

His fingers slide into my hair and his lips pause in front of mine. "Why did you really come here?"

"Because deep down inside I was hoping you didn't really move on from me."

"I didn't. I can't. I've tried so many times."

"Why would you do that if it doesn't feel wrong?" I rasp, holding him at a distance when he tries to bring his mouth closer.

"I did it for you. I tried for you. I thought it was the only way I could at least have my brother back."

I rub my nose over his, pressing our foreheads together. "You've always had me." I shove him back into the bathroom, closing the door behind us before pressing his back to the shower glass. "I've never stopped wanting to be yours in every way, and that's the problem."

"Is it?" His breaths are hot on my neck. "Because I don't see one. In fact, all problems disappear whenever I'm with you." He claims my mouth with his, thrusting his tongue alongside mine. His hand slides up my shirt, fingers pressing to my skin as he deepens the kiss and I lose myself in the warmth of his mouth. Breaths heavy and syncing together, our teeth clash. When his hand slides between us, reaching for my belt, I stop him, pushing at his chest with my palm.

"You have a fiancé."

His eyes blink rapidly, and he runs a hand through his hair. "I . . . That could be changed. I would never have said yes if you'd shown up sooner."

"I'm glad you did," I lie. "He's what you need. Not me. I do want to be in your life again but it shouldn't be like this."

"How should it be then? You watching me marry someone else and me picturing your face on my honeymoon?"

"You need a brother. That's what you need from me. You have him for everything else. You told him yes after all."

"Because you weren't here. Because I thought you were no longer an option."

"You need to keep thinking that way then. Because I'm not." I exit the bathroom, adjusting myself in my pants, and he stays where he is, not moving when I sit on the edge of his bed to stare at the hearts with our initials inside carved at the ends of his bed post. Not moving when I stand up and look toward the bathroom, waiting for him to walk out to argue with me some more.

Feeling like my feet are too heavy for the rest of my body, I stand in the doorway, and struggle to cross the threshold when I hear his cries echoing.

My heart twists, my chest caving from the pain. I'm doing this for him. I'm going to let him marry Glen and stop thinking of me in the wrong way. If I stay and entertain what we were doing in the bathroom again, that'll make me selfish, because I'll be keeping him all to myself again, for me.

This is what's right, and sometimes the best thing you can do will tear you apart before you learn to appreciate the outcome. I force one foot in front of the other, taking a deep breath as I walk into the next room.

He's right. My mom kept it exactly the same. The bedding, curtains, and System of The Down posters. Everything. Closing my eyes, I inhale the scent of him lingering everywhere around me. He really did come in here a lot. Often enough to leave so much of himself behind.

A hand rests on my arm and I crane my neck, my eyes held captive by his. They're wet and shining from the light breaking through the parting curtains. "Will you at least come stay with me? We can watch movies. Do brother stuff only. Just like you want."

"I . . . I don't know. I had a long flight here and didn't get much sleep last night."

"After all these years you're still a terrible liar. What about tomorrow?"

His bottom lip twitches and it was what he did when he knew I wasn't going to let him have his way easily. "Yeah, sure. Okay. Tomorrow only. I'll crash here after that. Then I can see if my Playstation still works."

"We can always take it to my house and try it there?" His voice trembles.

"Or we can play now while we wait for Mom?"

His lips shift from side to side and he nods. "Yeah, okay, but if you die before I do then you'll come stay with me tonight."

I sit next to him, reaching for the remote in his hand with my lips twisting. Not using words, I slump my shoulders in defeat, waving my head back and forth with a loud breath pushing out of my lips as I hit the "on" button on the TV remote.

A faint smile plays on his lips because he knows he's finally gotten his way, and it feels way too good letting him.

Twenty-Four

NATE

Jumping to my feet, I raise my hands in triumph. "Take that, sucker."

Barking out a laugh, Jace rolls his eyes and tosses his game controller beside him on the bed. "You always were a sore winner."

Doing a little dance in front of him, I shake my hips and stick out my tongue. "And you were always a sore loser."

Yanking me by the arm, he pulls me back onto the bed and tickles my side. We wrestle around, laughing and trying to one-up each other. My back hits the bed and he jumps on top of me, pinning down my chest when I try to sit up. "Now this is a game I've won every damn time."

"You joined the wrestling team in high school so it's an unfair advantage," I say dryly.

Flopping over to the other side of me, he rolls his head back and forth, smiling wide. "Who's the sore loser now?"

"I do learn from the best."

Elbowing me in the side, he stares up at the glow-in-the dark stickers, tilting his head. "You think those still work?"

"I know they do." I turn my face toward him. "Nothing beats the ones outside, though, and I have a pretty great view on my back porch."

"You're really set on me staying over tonight, aren't you?" He rubs at his chest, sliding close enough for our noses to touch when he fully looks my way. My breath catches in my throat, heart wild and all over the place in my chest. Neither of us move for a long time, our breaths matching and eyes locking.

"Boys? You in here?" Our mom's voice has us sitting up in bed and placing space between us.

Her eyebrows rise in alert when she peeks her head in, and a flashback to how she looked last time she walked in on us together takes hostage of my mind. I don't know why I'm waiting for her nose to turn up in disgust again and for disappointment to flash in her eyes when Jace nudges me back to reality.

Instead, her gaze is ping-ponging between the remotes Jace set in our laps without me noticing.

"Hey, Mom. We're just in here playing some video games," Jace says, forcing a smile.

"Oh," she says, not sounding fully convinced, as if somehow her eyes might be playing tricks on her. "It's good to know that thing still works. You left so much of your stuff behind, but I didn't want to get rid of it in case you missed it."

"Yeah, I saw. Feels like I've entered a time capsule. Thanks for saving it all. I've really missed being in here."

Her face softens, her hands moving to the front of her body. "Of course, hon. Feel free to take some of it back with you but don't feel obligated. We don't mind holding onto all y'alls old stuff. Helps the house feel less empty."

"Yeah. I'll take this with me for sure, and maybe some of my old comic books."

"What about those old pairs of white converse you could never part with?" I said pointedly.

"You mean the ones displaying your beautiful artwork," he says between laughs, and my mom watches us closely, fingers tugging at the hem of her shirt.

"You boys seem to be getting along like no time has passed between y'all. It's good to see." There's a hint of uneasiness in her voice. She's enjoying the brotherly exchange but worries it will eventually lead to more if Jace stays too long. Her thoughts are louder than she realizes, echoing around her in the form of uncomfortable silence.

"Yeah. I guess we are. It was only a matter of time before we found our way back, I guess. Especially being back in here surrounded by so many memories." Jace rubs his palms over his knees, stretching out his legs.

"Yeah, well, dinner will be ready in an hour. Would you two like to come help prepare everything for the salad?"

"Sure." Jace quickly gets to his feet, wasting no time taking the out she gives him.

"Yeah, whatever you need," I say in agreement, setting my control next to his.

Jace follows her out first and I'm right behind them, turning off the light before shutting the door. Mom ensures we're never alone for the remainder of the evening, giving us different tasks in the kitchen after dinner. Jace loads the dishwasher and I wipe down the table, before suggesting we watch a movie.

"Sounds like a good idea to me," Dad says, from the living-room couch, glancing back at us.

"Yeah, sure. It's been so long since we've had a movie night." Mom's face lights up and she grabs both of her hands, eyes shifting between us. "It's really good to have both my boys here. I definitely needed it this week."

Jace's eyebrows bunch together. "Everything okay?"

"It will be, I'm sure. Your aunt Tracy has just been in and out of the hospital, struggling with her MS. It's been hard on her whole family, and with Dan leaving—"

"Leaving? Are they getting a divorce?"

Mom nods solemnly. "Yeah. I guess her being sick all the time is too much for him. She can't travel as much as she used to and had to cut hours at work recently."

"I always knew that guy was a prick," Jace mutters.

"I think everyone did," I quip.

"Are we going to keep talking about sad stuff or are we going to finish enjoying our movie night?" Dad lifts his head, pressing a hand to the back cushion of the couch. "It's not like we get to see Jace often."

"He's right." Mom squeezes our fingers, pulling away. "You two go help your dad settle on a movie and I'll make the popcorn."

Doing what she asks, we head to where Dad is, and sit on opposite sides of him. Mom takes a seat in the recliner and we finally decide on the latest *Venom* movie. Dad's snoring fills the room halfway through and Mom sighs, getting up from her seat. "I guess I need to get that one to bed, before I have to hear him cry about the crick in his neck for a week straight from sleeping in that position for too long."

"You coming back?" I ask, tossing popcorn into my mouth.

"I think I'll turn in too, actually. Have an early day at the office tomorrow. You boys stay and finish the movie. If it gets too late, you can just crash in your old rooms."

"Dinner tomorrow again?" Jace settles the almost-empty bowl in his lap and Mom smiles.

"Yeah. I'd like that. I'm sure Dad would too. Night, boys."

"Night, Mom," we say in unison.

Jace's attention is back on the movie when Mom disappears to her room with a half-asleep Dad on her heels. Jace shakes the kernels in the bowl and I laugh, taking the bowl from him.

"More popcorn?"

"I can make it." He places his hand on the bowl, and I place a hand on his.

"Nah. I've got it. I used to be the snack runner, remember?"

"Only when we were home. You made me walk out to the stands whenever we went to the drive-in."

"That's 'cause I know how much you enjoy outdoor walks," I tease, and that drags a snort out of him.

"Whatever. Hurry up and see if we got any hot Cheetos in the pantry."

"Someone's sounding at home finally." I nudge him with my shoulder and stand up from the couch.

"Yeah, I guess having you here really helps."

Giddy inside, I smile all the way to the kitchen. We eat more popcorn and he tries to get me to eat one of his Cheetos. I don't tell him why we have them. I lied to Mom about them being from a friend who often brought extra food from home, because I didn't want her to know the truth of where they came from either. I've been saving them all this time. Whenever I visit our favorite sandwich place alone, I grab a bag with my meal, and I brought them here this morning when I knew he was coming over for dinner.

The movie reaches the credits and we stay on the couch talking about our last trip to the movies. Jace mentions how he has to watch scary movies alone now and shield his pillow's pretend eyes from jump scares.

Shaking my head, I laugh. "Oh, be quiet. You know I haven't even seen a horror flick since college."

"Really?" His forehead shifts in surprise. "Why not?" He slides a Cheeto between his reddening lips.

"Glen doesn't care for them and I don't really have anyone to watch them with. All my friends from work and school always choose some chick flick or drama when we meet at the theater."

"That sucks. I guess we'll have to watch one before I leave then."

"You'll still have to shield me from the scary scenes, though. Sure you're up for the task?"

He preens. "I think I can handle it."

Both deciding it's too late to drive anywhere, we turn in, walking into our separate rooms after telling each other goodnight in the dark hallway.

"See you in the morning," I say. "I hope you missed my famous pancakes."

"You mean the lopsided ones with slightly burned edges?" he says, pausing in the doorway.

"Hey, I'd like to think I've improved a little."

"Well, if it's only a little then I can't wait." He enters his room fully, leaving me alone, and I watch his closed door for too long before climbing into bed.

Shifting under the covers, I move around my pillows, unable to close my eyes for longer than a few seconds at a time. I stare up at the ceiling, reminiscing about the made-up stories Jace used to tell me when I couldn't sleep, replaying one of my favorites in my head until I relax enough to close my eyes again. As I'm dozing off, a high-pitched scream has me jolting up in bed. When Jace starts shouting unintelligible words in his sleep, I lock my door and rush to his room through our shared bathroom.

He's tossing and turning, drenched in sweat when I turn on the small lamp on his dresser. His eyes don't open and he shakes, saying, "No. I didn't do it. I was the one who stopped it. It couldn't have been me."

"Jace." I shake at his shoulder, watching his door. "It's okay. I'm here. You're only dreaming." His nightmares have stopped. "Jace," I say again and he swings at me, saying something under his breath.

"I tried to stop it," he cries. "I'm sorry I was too late. I tried."

My heart rattles in my chest. When I don't hear any noise out in the hallway, I move quickly to the door to twist the lock in place.

Jace cries some more, tugging at the pillows and slamming his legs against the bed. He slaps at his own face and scratches at his neck. I rush toward him, holding his wrists in place and kissing his temple. "Shh." I start singing an old lullaby, one that used to settle him the most on his worst days, and release him when his body goes slack.

Shutting off the lamp behind me, I crawl into bed beside him and wrap my arms tightly around him. I hold him as he tries to fight some more, singing louder until his breathing evens out. Finally he stills against me, and I bury my face in his neck and kiss his sweaty skin. He'd see this as a hardship, but I see it as being here for him like he's been for me. What's been a real hardship is spending the last seven years in a bed without him.

Twenty-Five

JACE

The strong scent of buttermilk pancakes assaults my nose and I sit up in bed, stretching my arms. The blanket lowers to my knees with one shove of my hands and my bare feet come in contact with the cold floor.

Pans bang together downstairs and I stand up, searching for my jeans. After throwing on enough clothes and running my fingers through my hair, I follow the alluring smell downstairs to where Nate is flipping pancakes on a large skillet while swinging his hips from side to side in the lightning bug pajama pants I didn't think he still owned.

They look better on him now than they did when he used to sneak into my bed during the first weeks of summer. Something I didn't think was possible. He fills them out well with his thick hips, round ass, and slender waist. His bare back is on full display, an array of freckles scattered along his fair skin.

What a damn sight he is, and it's all for me today. Dread quickly fills me when I remember Glen gets to have this whenever he wants, because

Nate is his now and will never be mine again. I can look but I should never touch, though I doubt I'll be able to stop if I ever get that close to him again. Actually, I know I won't.

Him getting out of bed this morning before me was a blessing. I was too much in a daze, drunk on sleep, to wrap my arms back around him. To memorize myself with his body again and ask him to help me make the world spin for old times' sake.

His sweet voice lulled me back to sleep and the nightmares faded away, and all I felt was him. I forgot how wonderful it was to feel his warm body pressed to mine. To feel his face nudge against my neck like no one else was meant to fit with him this way but me.

It isn't until I get closer that I notice the earbuds in his ears as he plates the pancakes, singing "Wannabe" by the Spice Girls at the top of his lungs. He turns his head enough to spot me behind him and his body stiffens, a beautiful blush creeping over his cheeks.

"Morning," he says, yanking the earbuds from his ears.

"Don't stop the dance and singing party on my account."

Lowering his head, the pink on his cheeks spreads to his chest. "I'll be happy to continue it if you join me."

"I don't know, watching was much more fun." I flit my gaze up and down the front of his body, unable to help myself. I can look but I can't touch. If I repeat those words to myself enough, maybe I'll keep listening. He's so damn tempting, though. And judging by the smirk playing on his lips, he's well aware.

"Well, as much as I love putting on shows for all my beloved fans, we have a showing to get to at one o'clock, and you sleeping in so late is kind of putting us behind."

I search the time on the stove, eyes bulging. "It's already past ten? How?"

"I'm guessing you're not getting enough sleep at the farm. Sit, so we can devour these pancakes and get ready."

I pull out and then stop dead in my tracks. "Wait . . . What showing? What are you getting me into today? Do you not have to work?"

"Nope," he says, excitement raising his voice as he sets our breakfast on the table. Our plates sit mere inches from each other and he walks around the corner to sit next to me. "I took the day off and rescheduled my two appointments for Monday. Oh, and I bought us tickets for the dollar theater. It's not the drive-in but they are playing *Texas Chainsaw Massacre*. They play a lot of older movies every Friday."

"Which one?" I take my seat next to him and he shuffles closer to me, scooting himself over further when I try to add more distance between us.

"Um . . . the latest one I think." He stabs his fork into his food, pressing his thigh to mine. I give up trying to move away, and settle against him, feeling as satisfied from the closeness as he looks when he wiggles beside me. "I think it's called *Leatherface*."

"Oh. Like when he's younger, or whatever."

"Yeah. I haven't seen it yet."

"I figured as much." I scoot my plate closer to me as I drown my pancakes in syrup. "You did say you hadn't seen any horror films since college, and there's actually a movie after it that came out in 2022."

"Of course you would know. I'm guessing you've seen it then?"

"Nah. I don't watch a lot of movies these days." It's not the same without you, I almost say, stopping myself before the words can fly out of my mouth.

"Then, what do you do? Go for joy rides on the tractor? Play corn hole?"

I laugh, licking sticky sweetness from my lips. "No. I mean, sometimes," I joke, shooting him a wink. "I read. Go for a swim in the pond. Take the horses for a ride. Visit the local book store and fish."

His eyes light up in wonder. "I've never ridden a horse before."

"And you're definitely missing out. They really are great animals." I shove a fork full of food into my mouth and he sets his fork down, leaning on his open palm and gazing at me dreamily.

"You should invite me out to your house sometimes so you can take me. Then I wouldn't have to miss out."

"Yeah." My fork scrapes against the plate as I miss my food. "Maybe after the wedding you can come down with Glen."

He leans back, eyes pointing down. "Yeah. Me and Glen."

Eating takes longer than planned with all the talking we do, but once I say the wrong thing, we're back to devouring our food in silence. Only the clinking sounds of dishes and our soft breathing fills the kitchen as we clean up our mess.

"You want to take a shower first?" I ask, stopping in front of the steps.

"Doesn't matter to me. You can go. I need to make a phone call real quick."

"Yeah, alright." I head up the stairs, hating the devastated sound in his voice. Was it the mention of Glen coming to visit too? He is his fiancé. Why wouldn't he want the love of his life with him when he travels? Glen being there would guarantee I wouldn't cross the line. Having him there would mean spending less time alone with Nate, because it wouldn't take long to be alone with him for me to fold.

Steam wraps around me as I turn the water on hot and slide the glass door open more. Shedding my clothes, I grab a washcloth from the drawer, and step into the tub. A shiver comes over me from the cool air following me from outside the shower, and I rush under the welcoming stream, lifting my face under the soft pressure.

A whoosh of cool air sweeps behind me and I freeze when the door closes. I don't recall it opening—I must've been too lost in how relaxed my body felt under the water. Soft footsteps move closer behind me and a hand settles on my hip.

"I thought we could save on water." Reaching around me, he grabs the wash rag from my hand and squirts soap onto it. With a steady hand he runs the rough material down my back and along my hip. My breaths are loud and heavy and I watch his every move as he slowly gets me clean.

I can't move anything other than my eyes, my lips sticking together when I try to speak. My cock stiffens when the towel runs over the base, swelling at the tip.

His breathing picks up too, hands shaking now as he runs his hand up and down in agonizing motions.

A moan cuts past my lips, slightly breaking them apart, but the space is too small for words to get through. My tongue sticks to the roof of my mouth, throat dry as he moves to my balls. He presses hard, his fingers touching parts of my skin between the towel.

"We did a good thing today, don't you think? Saving on water? Washing the extra dishes I left behind this morning when I was running late for work? We both deserve a reward."

It's been so long since I've had a reward like this. Usually it's the satisfaction I get from drawing out the pain of bad men—hearing their screams over a course of days and seeing how much I can make them bleed without killing them. I've missed his rewards. I've missed returning the favor too, and making a game of who can make who feel better. It was always a fucking tie.

His fingers wrap around my cock and he turns my body around, pushing me to the wall. Licking at my mouth, he closes the distance between us and rocks his cock over mine. Our moans overlap and he increases the thrusts of his hips, clasping his fingers around us both, squeezing at both of our bases.

"Nate," I warn.

"I'll stop messaging you after you leave Monday morning. I won't try to visit you or invite you to my wedding. I won't ask you to come back here or be a part of any more important moments. I'll marry Glen and learn to love him. But you have to do something for me first."

"What's that?" I gasp as the perfect amount of friction burns between us, creating delicious tingles along my skin. Each brush sets my skin alive and it's hard to focus on his words. I almost think he's doing it on purpose. Choosing the most inconvenient time to make a compromise.

"Give me what we had before you left . . . for the next two days. I want the chance to say goodbye properly. I didn't get to last time. It was taken from us. Can you give me that?"

"I . . . You'll really be okay with me never coming back? You'll really give me up and try to live your life without me?"

"Yes. But only if you agree to my deal. Only if you can treat me like nothing has changed for the remaining time you're here."

"I can do that, and when we say goodbye, that's it. You go on and live your life with your wonderful fiancé, while I return to the farm." Without you. My stomach plummets. He says he can do it and sounds so damn sure. He's giving me what I want. Only, it's not really what I want but what's best for him. This is for him, I tell myself again. *For him.*

"Okay."

I look deeper into his eyes, getting closer to my orgasm as I chase my waves of pleasure. "You'll really be able to hold your end of the bargain? No more text messages? Not even if you get the slightest urge to tell me what you're thinking?"

"Yeah. I'll get a journal."

I laugh, tilting his head back and wrapping my fingers around his slender neck as I crash my lips to his. And this right here is for me.

"Come for me, baby."

Nate let's go on a cry and I shoot my cum between us right after him, moaning into his hot mouth. His eyes roll into the back of his head, legs wobbling, and I wrap my arms around his waist to steady him on his feet.

"Ready to distract me on the way to the theater?"

"Yes, and I'm ready for you to kiss me in the row instead of me hiding in your shoulder during the scary scenes."

"I can do that."

I get him clean and we rinse off under the water before stepping onto the cold tile. Waiting for me on the small rug, he holds his arms down at his sides while I wrap a large towel around him. I kiss him again and we dress in clean clothes, constantly touching on our way to the car.

He's right, we do deserve a better goodbye than what we got. And this time we'll get it, because this is something I know I must do for us.

Twenty-Six

NATE

Jace does everything he promises he'll do—everything he used to do before we were torn apart. He holds my hand on the way to the theater, singing with me to all our favorite songs from that summer. He distracts me with kisses whenever a scene is too gory or scary. I don't need to hide from them as much as I used to, not with how safe I feel secured in his large arms, and with his strong scent flooding my nose.

We share a Slurpee and our hands occasionally bump each other as we reach for the popcorn. I get his smiles again. His laughter. I get him. It really will hurt when he leaves me again but we have a deal. I'll have to learn to get past it—I've done it before—but it feels so much harder this time, like I'm about to lose more of myself.

"What did you think of the movie?" He swings an arm around me, steering me toward the parking lot.

His fear of cars has been nowhere to be found. At least, it's what he wants me to believe, and he's doing a good job at hiding the truth if this really is some act of his. I don't think so, though. There are many things he handles easier now that so much time has passed. No guilt is visible in his eyes when he drinks a Coke. He doesn't second guess shoving handfuls of candy in his mouth and the dark areas of the parking lot don't faze him.

It makes me smile at how much he's healed. Has our being apart really been for the better? He's getting along just fine without me—better even. My stomach knots. He's right, isn't he? Going our separate ways is the right step to take. But fuck, it's painful. I'm dreading the day he walks out of my life again.

"It was good," I finally answer before hopping into the driver's side. "Did you like it?"

"Yeah. It was entertaining enough. Although that twist was a little annoying."

"Sometimes they can be. I kind of figured which one was supposed to be him, though. Expect the unexpected."

He laughs, nodding and strapping on his seatbelt as he settles beside me. "I can't believe you still have the same car."

"She still runs perfectly so why wouldn't I?"

His shoulders lift one at a time. "I don't know but I'm glad you do. I've missed being in here with you. I've missed being everywhere with you."

"Yeah me too." I lock my fingers around his, smiling lazily. "Where should we go to next?"

He looks up, rolling his head against the seat before meeting my eyes again. "Ice cream?"

A smile forms on my lips and I drive out of the parking lot. "Sounds perfect. I could go for some more sugar today."

"Me too," he says, wagging his eyebrows, and lays a quick kiss on my lips for the brief second I have my head turned.

His fingers stay intertwined with mine the whole drive, and I hate when our hands separate for the short time it takes for us to get out of the car.

But my hand is quickly being swept up by his as soon as we both step onto the sidewalk. He holds the door open for both of us, and relief washes over me at how empty the place is. Fewer prying eyes.

We order our ice cream—his three scoops and my two—and with our cups in our hands, we find a table that's kind of hidden out of sight. Whenever more people start swarming in, he drops my hand and links his ankle around mine. I smile, shoving a spoonful of ice cream between my lips.

As I'm swallowing down my last bite, he reaches over and wipes the corner of my mouth with his thumb. "Still can't keep your food in your mouth, huh?"

"No, but that's what I have you here for." I wink. "Feel free to wipe my mouth later tonight too, in case there are other things I can't keep in my mouth." I bat my lashes and he sputters a laugh.

"Still got that dirty mouth too."

"What? I was talking about when we have dinner."

"Sure you were. I want to kiss you so bad right now."

"Then take me home so you can do it as much as you want." My breaths stutter.

"Your house?"

"Yes. More privacy there. We don't have to worry about Mom walking in on us again either."

Heat reddens his cheeks and he ducks his head. "You just had to bring that up, huh?"

"You know you've been worried about the same thing."

He sighs. "Maybe a little. She's finally acting somewhat normal around me. Not sure I'd get that back a second time."

"You're her son and she loves you. She'll always want to be there for you. You should have seen how many times she looked at her phone when she was waiting for your calls. She always had the biggest smile as soon as she heard your voice on the other end."

His lips shake a little. "You're not only telling me what you think I want to hear so I can feel better, are you?"

"No." I rest both arms on the table, leaning forward. "I'm telling you what you need to hear. Now let's get out or here so I can see what rocky road tastes like on your lips."

I get a little sample of him mixed with ice cream in the car, and again when he shoves me against the wall next to my front door. The keys nearly fall from my hand as his mouth travels over my lips. I don't care who sees us. We could be broadcasted on TV right now and I wouldn't stop.

He only stops long enough for me to get the door open and shoves me inside, attacking my mouth again. Laughing against his ravenous mouth, I kick the door closed behind me and he leads me to the couch.

With all his weight on top of me, he pulls off my shirt and then his. He takes a brief look around, smiling. "So this is where you live? I expected everything to be more bright and loud in color."

"You haven't seen the bedroom yet," I grin and he laughs, stroking one of my nipples.

"I'll let you give me the grand tour later. Right now I want to recreate a first that should only have stayed between us. Not because I'm ashamed, but because I don't want to share anything between us with anyone else."

"I don't think we can add greed to the list."

He huffs, tugging on my hard nub. "What about generosity? Selfishness? But what I'm about to make you feel should fit all those categories."

My breath hilts. "You'll have to do it first before it can count."

A sexy smirk plays on his lips and it's so damn sinful, but nothing compared to his hands that won't stop exploring my body as if it's their first visit.

"Let's not waste any more time then."

Licking his way down to my belly button, he tugs down my pants and underwear in one swoop, rubbing his nose in the dark hair around my stiffening cock.

"So damn sexy." He traces the veins on my shaft with the tip of his tongue, working his way to my leaking tip. "I've missed tasting you here."

His tongue swipes over a bead of precum and his deep groan is like fire under my skin. "And here."

"Here too." He lowers his head to my balls, sucking each one into his mouth as he strokes my cock.

"Especially here." He rubs a finger over my twitching hole and lifts me by my hips to bury his face between my cheeks. His moans vibrate against my hole, adding to the delicious pleasure I'm getting from his sucking mouth.

His tongue thrusts inside me, tasting me everywhere it reaches and making my body tremble.

I rotate my hips, pressing my ass harder to his face as he licks deeper. Adding a finger, he swirls his tongue around it while giving my cock more hard tugs.

My nails sink into the cushion and I close my eyes, holding back the erupting pleasure inside me. I'm waiting for him to say the magic words—for him to let me know he's ready for me to let go. I didn't realize how much I'd longed for this until earlier in the shower. Glen never edges me like this. He never sets my soul alive the way this man can while also having me combust at the seams.

Maybe it's a bad idea to know what I've been missing. To get a taste of what could be mine if things were different. My body tenses against the couch as he continues to drive me out of my skin with his hands and mouth. I'm his to do with as he pleases. To play with however he wants. Those thoughts alone have my hole pulsating and cock twitching. I'm not sure how much time passes while he's feasting on my hole and plunging his fingers into me.

All I know is when he's finally shoving his cock inside me my body lights up, inviting him in, inch by delicious inch.

"Please," I beg. "I need—"

"I know what you need. To have someone else guide you. To make me proud by being so damn good. So damn patient."

"Yes," I squeak, wiggling beneath him as he pulls out his cock only to slam it back in harder and faster. He doesn't take long to find my sweet spot, listening to my body better than anyone else has. He rolls his hips, circling my prostate with his tip before going back to moving in and out. Stars shoot across my closed lids as he grinds his cock, hitting me in all the right places.

"Fuck," I scream and he kisses my neck, trailing his lips to my parting mouth.

"So perfect for me. You're doing so good. Just a little more."

Lifting my ass high, he slams his hips forward, coming on a grunt. Warm liquid fills my hole and he goes back to palming my cock while using my squeezing hole to milk himself. I flail my arms, tears streaming from my eyes, and low whines slip from my lips.

I move my hips in sync with his hand and his lips tickle my ear, whispering, "Give me your cum, baby. Give me more of you to taste."

My body spasms at his words and I sink into the imploding pleasure, drowning myself in it until my whole world is tilting. His warm lips claim mine, our mouths moving lazily against each other.

"You did amazing, little brother. You're so damn perfect and all mine right now. Not Glen's or anyone else's. Only mine."

My heart sings, feeling elated, full. If only this wasn't temporary. If only we weren't on our way to our last goodbye. We lie tangled in each other, sweaty and sticky. My mom calls to tell us she and Dad can't make dinner after all and will have to reschedule for tomorrow. As she's saying her goodbyes, Jace starts licking me clean, swiping his tongue over the leftover cum on my skin.

I bite my lower lip to keep from moaning when he laps his tongue around my spent cock.

"Yeah. We'll see you tomorrow. That's okay, Mom. We'll go out somewhere together. Maybe the taco truck we used to eat at during the summer." I send him a glare when he sucks my tip into his mouth, grinning around me.

"Love you too. Bye."

I hang up the phone and toss it on the coffee table. "You're an asshole."

"What? I helped you get clean so you could add more to that list of yours. I want to help you fill up a whole page before I leave, so I have so many good things to read over on my trip home."

"You could have waited until I got off the phone," I huff.

"Oh, you were on the phone? I didn't notice." He grins up at me, running his nose over my inner thigh.

"Yeah, okay. I'm hungry and we no longer have dinner plans."

"I can cook us something."

I guide his body up higher, kissing his lips sweetly. "No. I'm not ready to separate from you yet. Let's order delivery. Chinese or pizza?"

"How about Texas Roadhouse? I miss those buttery rolls." He rubs his stubble over my chin.

"Sure. I haven't had those in forever."

Stretching out my arm, I grab my phone and search for the number. I order food and we laze on the couch, sharing an infinite amount of kisses until the food arrives.

A loud knock has Jace scrambling from the couch, and I laugh when he ties a throw blanket around his waist to answer the door. With food in hand, he walks back over to me, shaking his hips so hard the blanket falls to the floor, and I fall back on the couch in a heap of laughter.

We move to the table to eat our food, Jace dragging my chair closer to his. His foot rubs over the top of mine, and we can't fully stop touching each other in some way. He helps me clean up, rubbing his hand up and down my back as we make our way back to the couch.

We get lost in each other's bodies again, Jace teasing me for hours before letting me come again. Worn out and loving where I am too much, I cozy up to his chest and drift off, saving the rest of the house tour for tomorrow.

Twenty-Seven

JACE

Morning light casts shadows on Nate's back. I don't have to worry about waking up next to him this time. I don't have to worry about him getting out of bed before me. He makes a soft sound when I make shapes out of his freckles with my fingers.

His eyes twitch, lashes fluttering, and he presses his face to my chest. "Mm, morning."

"Morning." I brush a curling strand of hair from his face and kiss his nose.

"What time is it?" he asks between yawns, placing his leg on top of mine.

"No idea." My stomach groans and I glance between us. "Food time."

His laughter tickles my chest. "I think I'm in the mood for donuts." His eyes flick up at me.

"You saying you want to go to the bakery down the street?"

He shakes his head. "No. I want to have some delivered and stay on this couch with you for as long as I can."

"You mean until dinner and our parents."

He stifles a groan, shifting to his back and pushing me more to the edge. "Don't remind me."

"You wanted it to be like old times." I purse my lips and he elbows me in the chest.

"Yeah, except for the part where I had to wait hours for us to be alone so I could kiss you."

"No one said anything about hours." I trace the seam of his lips with my thumb, kissing his forehead. "I'll put the order in this time." I search around us, lifting my pants from the ground and swiping my phone from my pocket. There's a missed call from an unknown number waiting for me.

"What is it?" Nate lifts himself halfway up on his elbows, looking between my questioning face and the screen.

"Some number I don't know. Probably a scam call." Twisting my body, I place my feet on the ground and throw on my pants.

"I like the throw blanket better," he says, smiling up at me with a little bit of beard burn on his neck and other random places on his body. Will Glen see all the marks I've left behind? Why do I suddenly have the urge to make more?

Shaking off the thought, I lower my face to peck his sweet mouth. "And I'll freeze my ass off less in these and get fewer weird looks from the delivery person."

"Okay fine, but when it's just us, I don't want you wearing anything at all."

"Does that mean you won't either?"

He stretches his arms up above his head, giving me a cheeky grin. "Yes. We'll put on clothes to have dinner and then we'll immediately take them off once we walk back through that door."

"Sounds like you got the rest of our day together all figured out."

His lips turn downward and I hate myself for mentioning it too. This is our last day together, so we have to make it count. I fly out tomorrow afternoon and he's going to want to kiss me at the gate, playing out a scene from one of those romantic comedies he'd ask me to watch after we'd seen a movie he found to be too scary.

After deleting the missed call, another one comes in from the same number and I hit ignore. If they call again, I'll probably hit the block button. I don't give my number to a lot of people. Swiping to the Uber Eats app, I place our food order, adding lots of extra rolls, and throw myself back on the couch. Nate and I roll around, kissing until we're both out of breath and flushing.

His swelling cock digs into my clothed hip and I count the minutes until the food gets here. Quickly slamming the door shut as I send my tip, I set the donuts on the coffee table and take off my pants.

Loud giggling is forced out of him when I jump on him, rubbing my naked body against his. My leaking cock leaves a trail behind on his hip and I smear it into his skin. Head tilted back, his eyes flutter and he ruts against me, making addicting needy sounds.

His moans are muffled with my mouth as I dip my tongue between his lips. "We should eat something."

"Yeah, we should." He goes back to assaulting my mouth with his tongue and I circle my fingers around his nipples, teasing the area and never actually coming in contact with the darker skin.

"We really should," I say, climbing off him and he sticks his arms out, puffing his bottom lip in a pout.

"We'll eat, shower, and then you'll give me that tour you promised me yesterday." I hand him a donut and he downcasts his eyes.

"Fine. Or how about tour first and then shower?"

"Either order works for me. As long as they both come after much needed sustenance."

He sinks his teeth into the powdered dough, moaning around it. I can't believe I'm jealous of a donut. Glen's one thing, but food? I want the pleasure of pulling those sounds from him to be mine alone.

White power dusts his lips, and I do what I'd wanted to at the ice-cream shop, sliding close enough to lick them clean.

He purposely covers his lips in jelly and sugar as he eats his last donut, tempting my mouth some more. I eat my kolache and grab us both water from the fridge to chase our food down with, and we share more kisses on the couch before he shows me the guest room where I was supposed to be sleeping. It's filled with softs blues and greens. I laugh when we enter his room next—nothing about it is subtle.

Bright, colorful artwork lines the walls, and there are red curtains with matching bedding. Zebra-striped throw pillows are scattered on top, and don't get me started on his polka-dotted chair.

"Why does it look like a circus threw up in here?"

We both burst out in laughter, tumbling together onto the bed. After wrinkling and dirtying his bedding, I sit on his obnoxious chair while he rides my cock, but I don't drag either of our orgasms out this time, desperate to see more of my cum dripping from his hole. He comes before me, bouncing up and down while sounding exasperated.

I push my hips upward, arching up until I'm deeper and surrounded completely by his warmth. He cries out from being too sensitized, digging his nails into my shoulders as I finish using his tight channel to get off.

He slumps against me as I come, grinding slowly as I lose myself in each sensation racking through my body.

"Got any more rooms for me to see?"

A laugh pushes past his lips and he kisses me. It's slow and patient. That's exactly how loving him has felt. Long-lasting and with no end in sight. Blocking my view of him never lessened it before, so why do I think it'll work this time?

"Can one of you boys get me the flour?"

"Sure," I clip, marching toward the pantry.

Her next words are hard to make out when I get too far away, but I hear Nate say, "Don't worry, Mom, I'll get it."

The door to the pantry taps closed behind me and Nate greets me with a large mischievous smile.

"What are you doing?" I grab for the tall container labeled flour from the second shelf.

"Getting the sugar Mom asked for once you were already out of sight. And getting my kiss."

Balancing the container in one arm, I step forward and brush my lips over his. They lock together, tongues fighting to let go, but I press my hand to his chest when he tries to dive in for more. "We should get this stuff to the kitchen before she suspects something."

He groans. "Fine." And snakes an arm behind me to grab the sugar. Mom's mixing something in a bowl when we return, and Dad's laughing at something on the TV. He joins us in the kitchen when Mom asks him to set the table, and sits with Nate and me at the table, chit-chatting while we wait for the food to be done.

Mom brings everything to the table and looks between me and Nate when she sees us sitting close together. Nate kicks his foot against mine, reaching under the table to link his pinkie with mine in between clearing his plate. Whenever he thinks our parents aren't paying attention, he shoots me a flirty glance and slides his hand deeper into mine.

Dad suggests another movie night and we all remind him how bad he is at them. "I think we need to have a movie day with you," I say.

"He'll fall asleep during those too," Mom says, dabbing her mouth with a napkin.

The kitchen fills with laughter and everything really does feel like before. I enjoy it while it lasts, suggesting we eat our dessert on the back patio. Outside, we share more laughter and exchange stories under the stars.

Dad is the first to turn in and then Mom, leaving me and Nate alone, leaning into each other. After making sure the coast is clear, he sneaks in a kiss and we walk over to the old tree house. The ladder is a little wobbly, and I swear I see my life flash before my eyes when I step on a loose board once inside.

Nate scoots around me, sitting down on the old mattress and reaching for the old games. "I can't believe this is all still up here."

"Yeah, and it looks like some wildlife got in," I say, pointing to the box of twinkies with bite marks in it.

Nate wrinkles his nose, pushing it back with a stick, and jumps back when his phone rings. "Shit." His eyes widen when he glances down at the screen. "Glen. I forgot I was supposed to call him back last night."

"Why don't you talk to him now?" I suggest, hoping he doesn't listen.

He nibbles on his bottom lip, hitting the answer button and pressing the phone to his ear. "Hey, handsome."

I cringe on the inside, trying not to show my feelings of disgust and jealousy on my face. I pretend to go back to looking at everything we left in here all those summers ago, and Nate looks away from me, scrubbing at his face.

"I can't wait to see you either. Yeah, sure." He sighs softly, poking at a small hole in the blanket underneath him. "I will. How's work?"

His eyes move from side to side as he leans back, supporting his weight with his other hand. "That's good."

Hating how Glen is cutting into the last few hours I have with Nate, I decide I won't let him take any more. After all, he's about to take everything from me again soon. Crawling forward, I yank on Nate's shorts and he lifts his hips, not fighting me as I place my face between his thighs. I lick at the wet spot on his underwear.

He winces, slamming his foot forward when I push my tongue into the opening of his underwear to tease every bit of skin I can reach. He keeps giving his fiancé short answers while letting me have his body. Once the button is undone on the front, his cock springs free and I take it all the way down to the back of my throat. I bob my head up and down, smiling around the fullness in my mouth.

He gasps, squeezing his eyes shut as he breathes solely through his mouth.

"I love you too," he says, and the words are like nails on a chalkboard. Feeling primal and possessive of what feels like only mine right now, I yank the phone from his hand and hit end.

His eyes round, and when he tries to reach for it when it rings again, I toss it behind me after shutting it off.

"Why did you do that?"

"You can talk to your fiancé for the rest of your lives. All I get is now, and I'll be damned if I let him have that too."

I slide my mouth back down his length, running my tongue all over his sensitive spots. He thrusts his hips and I meet each swing of his hips, gagging when I'm choking him down. He moans, body shuddering as he tugs at my hair. His cock grows in my mouth and his hips press to the floor. As he's about to let go, I pull off him, and he looks at me as if I've splashed cold water on his face.

"Why'd you stop?"

"Tell me you love me."

"What?" His eyes are wild, hair mussed.

"Tell me you love me. The same way you did him, but I want you to mean it."

"You know how I feel, Jace."

"I want to hear it. Over and over as you come from my mouth."

"I . . . I love you," he says softly.

"Louder," I demand.

"I love you. God, I love you, Jace. I fucking love you." His words shift to long moaning when I go back to servicing his dick with my mouth, adding slight suction to the tip on my way up.

"I love you," he shouts, thrashing underneath me as he shoots down my constricting throat.

"I love you," he whispers. "Only you."

Pulling off with a pop, I lick my lips, collecting any missed drops from his skin. I place a kiss to his tip and crawl up his body, throat aching and heart sulking from the pain it can already feel from the blow that's about to come tomorrow.

"I know, baby." I say against his lips. "I know. I love you too."

I guess I get to have one thing more than Glen after all.

Twenty-Eight

NATE

He's leaving today. Forever. No one prepares you for moments like this. For the already-there hole in your heart to expand from having to let go of the person who showed it how to beat properly to begin with.

Jace runs a finger over my bottom lip. "Want to get something to eat before dropping me at the airport?"

I shake my head, scooting in closer. "Just lie here with me until it's time to go."

"For the whole two hours?"

"Yes," I rasp. "For as long as you can." Fighting back tears, I rub my face into his chest. I'd never gone looking for him at the farm, because Mom wouldn't tell me where it was at first, and when I finally learned the location I was afraid of him pushing me away when I showed up. I was worried it had been too long, and told myself I'd only go if he asked.

I waited for him. For him to write me back. For him to run to me. Now I'm waiting for him to leave, and soon I'll wait for my heart to fill the gap he leaves behind. I don't know if it'll ever happen. I don't think I can really let him go.

Tears hang at the corner of my eyes and I squeeze them tighter, wrapping an arm around him, wishing it was enough to hold him here forever. I thought I could make one last time be enough. It'll never be enough. I'll always want more. Always.

"Please don't go," I say against his skin. "Stay longer."

He rakes his fingers through my hair, pressing a kiss to the top of my head. "It's already been decided. You can't take back what we agreed upon after I've already held up my end of the bargain."

"I'll go with you then. If it has to do with you no longer wanting to be here and facing our family."

"No, baby." He sighs against me. "You belong here. Free of all the burdens I'll bring you."

"What burdens?" I peer up at him. "Your nightmares?"

"No. My nightmares are not the worst part of me."

"Then what? Whatever it is, we can work on it together."

"It's too late for that. I am who I am, and you are this bright light I never want to dim."

"But—"

"How about you let me hold you while we watch one last scary movie together?"

"I . . ." I lick my dry lips. "Okay."

I don't fight him on it anymore. A deal is a deal and I need to stand by it like I promised I would. I can try. I've gone through this before—only this time it feels more final.

He turns on the TV and chooses the movie when I don't make any suggestions. I go still against him, looking at the way his chest rises and falls while he watches the screen. When the alarm goes off on his phone, I help him load the trunk with his bags. Neither of us says a word at the restaurant, and I pull my hand away from his when he tries to hold it.

Saying goodbye this time will be different than it would have been back then. Because no one's making him go this time. He's leaving on his own. This is his choice to make and he's still settled on walking away from us. I help him get his bags out of the car, and when he tries to kiss me I press a hand to his chest. "How about you save that goodbye kiss for next time."

His face falters. "Oh, baby. This is it. There is only this time. Don't you want to make it count?"

I stand my ground, backing away. "Have a safe flight home, Jace. And if you want that kiss, you'll have to come back for it."

His eyes water and he takes a deep breath. "Bye, Nate. I love you, and in order to keep you loving me, we have to go our separate ways."

"I still don't understand. There's nothing you could do that would make me stop loving you."

"And the longer you think that, the better we'll all be. Maybe we'll both be in a better place in seven years. Maybe by then, we both can officially say we've moved on and you can really be the brother I should have kept you as."

He lifts his bags and disappears slowly into a crowd of people. I stand here, waiting for him to turn around, and I have no doubt in my mind I'll be waiting in seven more years as well.

Twenty-Eight

JACE

Heart heavy, I sit in my seat, waiting for the plane to take off. Something sharp digs into my leg from my book bag, and my breathing picks up when I pull out the notebook Nate made me when we were younger.

"All the things that make Jace a good person."

I stroke my fingers over the title before flipping through the pages. My lips stretch into a smile when I see the last list made was this morning.

Jace cares about others' needs before his own.
Jace showed me the world while I stood still.
Jace kept me safe from Leatherface.

I laugh and read on. Skimming the page until I reach the last one.

Jace thinks he's choosing what's right for me over what he wants.
Jace has always been what's right for me.

I shut the book and shove it back in my bag, staring out the window, seeing his words even when I shut my eyes.

I tried to be right for him. I tried to be right for myself but then blood covered my hands. Fearful eyes have been aimed toward me. What they say on the local news, about the man who goes around town mutilating men, are things I can't hear him say too.

Evil. Monster. Disturbed.

They don't care what those men did before I got to them. Not all of them had track records, and that's what made them more dangerous. No one was watching them. No one knew to keep others safe from their sick thoughts and actions. No one but me.

I hurt and destroy the lives of people who deserve it, but I'm still hurting people. I'm still dangerous. No matter what, that's still what everyone sees. It's all they'll ever see. But not him, and I'll do whatever it takes to let him only see the good sides of me.

Twenty-Nine

JACE

As soon as I exit the plane my phone rings and I answer without looking to see who it is, expecting to hear uncle Judd's voice on the other end. Who I hear instead has me stopping in the middle of a crowd, ears buzzing.

"Hey, son. It's been a while."

"Who is this?" Hairs stand at the back of my neck.

"I think you know."

"I'm sorry but you have the wrong number. Please don't call here again." I end the call, shoving my phone into my pocket, unable to move my feet. Everything spins around and I can't get his voice out of my head. I hear him as I walk to the baggage claim, when I wait outside in the big bright sun, and as I get into Uncle Judd's truck.

"So how was it?" He looks ahead, driving toward the road.

"Huh?" I say, feeling numb and too stuck in my head.

"The trip? How was the family? Your dad good?"

Dad. He means his brother, not the man who called me only minutes ago. How can I let him affect me so much? How does he have the ability to make me feel so damn small?

"I . . . good. Everyone's good." I rest my hands in my lap, watching as the cars move past us.

"You hungry? Your aunt made your favorite. Steak and potatoes."

I try to stay in the present, but it's not as easy to do with anyone who isn't Nate. He has a way of pulling me away from everyone and everything.

"Can't wait." I force a smile. "Sorry. Long flight and I didn't sleep much last night."

"Your mom said you were staying in a hotel. That's your first mistake there."

I push out an awkward laugh. "Yeah. You're probably right."

"People my age usually are." He shoots me a smile, turning up the radio. The guy in the song mentions how hard it is to walk away after being so close, and I resonate with him. It took everything in me not to go back, and then my dad called, reminding me of who I've become because of him. I'm not the monster he is, but the fact that the authorities have me listed as such makes me feel like I'm not safe enough for the man I love most in this world.

This is for him.

Those words have become my mantra and what has me blocking his number again as soon as I get home.

Thirty

NATE

"You hear about that man out where your uncle lives who's been torturing people in his cellar? Or is it a basement? Or maybe both."

A small laugh has my stomach shaking. "Don't worry. I'm sure he won't come after me in the short amount of time I plan on being there."

"You don't know that," Dad says.

"I think you watch too much news. Look, I'll call you and Mom when I get there. I'm sure Jace won't let anything happen to me."

"I'm sure you're right. See you when you get back."

The line goes quiet and I step forward when I see my ride pull up. "You Nate?" he asks through the cracked window.

"Yeah." I put my bag in the trunk and climb in the back seat.

"You're aware how far we have to go, right?" He peers at me through the rearview mirror.

"Yeah." I sit up taller, adjusting my shirt.

"Like, this place is really out in the sticks."

"I'm aware," I say lowly, meeting his gaze.

"Alright. Just making sure."

I check my messages, flipping over to a game when I need something to distract me from the bubbles in my stomach. Am I really doing this? I close my eyes, envisioning Jace helping me onto a horse while never letting go of my hand. Yes, I am.

I tried to stick to my end of the deal, and I did for a little while, until I couldn't escape the scent he left behind in my bed and couch. I couldn't escape him. He was everywhere. In my dreams, in my photo gallery, the first name I thought of when I woke up.

It turns out, I really couldn't do it. But why should I when what we have is something most people could only wish for? I never even saw it coming. The best things in life come as a surprise, and Jace was definitely all of the above. I'll show up at his door and convince him to change his mind. I'll remind him I'm not perfect myself. I cheated on my fiancé and I'm willing to stomp all over his heart in order to find mine again.

On the last twenty minutes of my ride, I pull up the note app on my phone and start a new list. I title it, "All the things that make Nate a bad person."

Didn't go after the love of my life when I found out where he was.
Said yes to marrying a man I don't love.
Cheated on my fiancé.
Fell for my big brother.
Went against a deal I made with my best friend
Invited myself to someone's house without them knowing.
Is considering stealing a horse.

Sitting back in my seat, I hit save and exit the screen. Green grass and trees are everywhere. So many ponds, and cows too. I'm already loving the view out here. Very peaceful and quiet.

"Almost there," the guy says. "The one good thing about driving here is there's never any traffic. What I don't understand is why anyone would want to visit a place out in the middle of nowhere."

"It's not really for you to understand." I shift in my seat and wipe my sweaty palms on my jeans.

"Sorry, just trying to start a conversation."

And he can feel free to stop at any moment. We reach a long dirt road with only one house on it. Blue and white, exactly like all the pictures Dad showed me. Mom wouldn't tell me anything about where uncle Judd lived, but she wasn't going to stop me from finding out.

The car comes to a stop behind a blue pickup and the driver pops the trunk. "Well, here we are. My name's Andy and I work down at the Stop and Go, fifteen minutes that way if you ever need someone to show you around." He gives me a once over and my stomach recoils.

"Yeah, I think I'm good Andy, but thanks." I step out of the car and grab my bag. The front door opens and my aunt steps out on the porch, lifting her hand in front of her face.

I close the trunk and walk up the long dirt driveway as I wave Andy off. He couldn't even take me to the damn front of the house. I wonder if he would have if I'd taken him up on his town tour.

"Nate, is that you?" My aunt beams, rushing down the steps.

"Hey, Auntie. How are you?"

"Oh my goodness. I can't believe it. I haven't seen you since you were small. You know your uncle doesn't like to leave the state."

"I know." I smile, embracing her in a hug. She smells like freshly baked cookies and lilacs.

"I didn't know you were coming up for a visit. If I had, I would have been more prepared. Your brother didn't mention anything to me about it. I'll have to get on to him when he gets back."

"Oh, don't be mad at him. He didn't know. This is a surprise visit. He said I should come out and see the farm, so here I am. Sorry, I should have called."

"Oh, nonsense." She waves me off. "You know you're welcome here anytime. I would just have liked to fix the guest room for you, is all. Unless you'd rather sleep out in the barn with your brother."

"It doesn't matter to me where I sleep. I'll set a tent up outside if I have to."

She shoves at my chest. "Oh, stop. You know I'd never have you do that. Not unless you were out back deer hunting with your uncle."

"Yeah, I don't hunt so that's a no for me."

She laughs, leading me inside. "You can put your bag in your brother's room for now. I'll go make sure the guest room has clean bedding."

"It's really not a bother," I say and she shrugs me off, disappearing down a long hallway. The door snicks open and Jace walks in, holding a line of fish. "Dinner has arrived." He plasters a smile on his face but it quickly dies as soon as his eyes land on me.

"Nate?"

"Hey," I say, squeezing onto the handle of my bag.

"What are you doing here?"

I inch closer, checking around us to ensure we're alone. "I came to get that kiss. Only I want one every day."

"Nate." He presses his hand to my chest when I try to move closer. "You shouldn't be here. You made a promise."

"You did too, so I guess this means we both suck at those. We can call it even." I wrap my fingers around his hand. "I don't want to be without you anymore. I can't do another seven years. Please don't make me."

His eyes turn hazy. "You're really stubborn, you know that?" He tugs me closer, rubbing his nose over mine.

"I guess that's another thing we have in common then."

He blows out a breath. "I guess there's no walking away from you, is there?"

"No. At least not for too long."

He laughs. "Then I guess I better stay where I am."

"Yeah, I guess so. You can't resist me anyway, remember?"

He nods against me. "I remember. I remember very well." He tugs on my bottom lip with his teeth. "I see you're no longer wearing your ring." He looks down at my finger.

"No. Mom and Dad don't know yet. I asked him if we could wait to tell everyone. He agreed. But I think it's only because he thinks he can change my mind."

"Can he?" He takes a step back, studying my eyes.

"I don't think I'd be here if he could."

"So we're really going to do this?" He tugs at the bottom of my shirt, narrowing his eyes on me.

"Looks like it."

"What about your job and everything back home?"

"You are my home." I stand on my tiptoes and kiss his lips.

Loud footsteps have us breaking apart and I straighten my shirt, feeling the warmth Jace's hand left behind.

"Are you going to set those fish in the kitchen or keep parading them around?"

Jace's eyes grow big and he shakes his head. "Ah, must have forgotten what I was doing thanks to our surprise guest here."

"Oh, sure, blame me."

"I am." He grins, walking ahead of me, and our aunt follows us as we step into the kitchen.

"I got the room fixed up for you, hun, but feel free to sleep anywhere you'd like."

"Careful what you say, you might find this one sleeping with the new foal."

"Wait, you guys have a baby horse?" I say, jumping up in excitement.

My aunt laughs. "I'm pretty sure that will be on you, Jace, since he didn't even know such a thing existed until you said so."

"Oh, what do we have here? A full house." Uncle Judd walks in, looking between us all. "When did you get here, Nate?"

"Only like an hour ago."

"You going to help your brother clean those fish?" He points to the counter where Jace sets down a knife.

"I wouldn't know where to start, but I'm happy to be here for support."

Uncle Judd laughs, patting me on the back. "I'm glad you could make it out for a visit. It's been so long since we've seen you. Next time you should bring your dad with ya."

"I'll try. Dad loves the city, though."

"Oh, I know. I'm guessing you do too."

"It's alright, but I have a feeling I'm going to love the country more," I reply, smiling back at Jace.

Thirty-One

JACE

He's here. He's actually here. I was going to argue again, about why he shouldn't be, but then my hand touched his and I knew I was done before I started. Worry will forever sit at the back of my head, about whether he'll hate me when he finds my guest no one knows about in the shed out back, but I'm too far gone to step away again.

His smile is big and bright as he runs his hand down the mare's back. "She's beautiful. Is she yours?"

"Yeah." I hand him the brush and he brushes her hair, and his lips stretch even wider when she nudges his hand with her nose when he stops. "I think she likes you."

"The feeling is definitely mutual."

"It helps to establish some trust before taking her for a ride."

His face lights up. "I'll get to take her for a ride?"

"Yeah. I was thinking first thing in the morning."

He continues brushing her while I feed her an apple slice.

"I won't say no to that. Will I get to see more of the animals too?"

"Sure. You might retract that question when you meet the rams though," I say between chuckling.

"I can see why you like it out here so much." He drops his hand.

"I like it even more now." I grab his wrist, rubbing my thumb over the small scar on his skin. "I must have missed that before."

"Yeah, I cut it open on a piece of glass in the sink while I was washing dishes."

"You're still a danger to yourself, I see," I say humorously.

"Yeah. So that means I should be worried more about myself than you," he says smugly, kissing my lips. "You going to show me the place you go when you want to be alone?"

I inhale deeply when I nudge my nose into his cheek. "Sure, but if I do that now, we might miss dinner."

His eyes heat. "I had a big lunch at the airport anyway."

I laugh, sealing my lips over his and I drag him out of the stables. Sunlight hits our faces, and when I see no one else is out here, I continue holding his hand as I steer him toward the old barn. We push our way through the double doors and he jumps ahead of me, exploring the large space. He smiles up at the godawful curtains I took from our parents' house that are blocking off a section.

"They really were the perfect touch." I tug at them, looking at him lovingly.

"Yeah. They look really good here."

"And so do you." I shove him toward the futon, lowering him to the black mattress with me while capturing his lips. My tongue dips into his mouth and he fights for dominance as I slide a hand up the front of his shirt.

His face pulls back a little and he takes his shirt off, staring at the partly open doors. "Does anyone ever come out here?"

"No." I remove my shirt next and then undo his pants, my cock twitching when I see how wet he is for me, his cock leaking like a faucet already. Lowering myself, I drag my tongue along the damp spots and I suck him through the thin fabric.

His breaths hitch and he moans when I rip the center of his underwear, aggressively taking his cock in my hand while I lick my way back up his body. "Tell me what you want, baby."

"You. I just want you."

"And it's exactly what you'll get from now on. Are you this needy with anyone else?" I ask, loving how he turns to putty in my hands.

"No. No one else." He whimpers, writhing against my hand. "Please fuck me. I need you inside me. I need to have you in a place I never thought I'd get to."

I strip out of the remainder of my clothes, searching for lube on the nearby table. I squirt some in my hand, stroking my cock and slicking up his hole. He rolls his hips, rubbing himself on the tips of my finger as I push my way inside. "Fuck, you're so tight."

I go deeper, twisting around as I pass his tight ring of muscle. Adding another finger, I spread them both apart, scissoring inside him until I feel he's ready for me.

"So fucking hungry for me, aren't you, baby?"

"Yes."

"I love being inside this slutty little hole. My slutty hole."

"All yours," he says, arching his hips. "Only yours."

"Yes, only mine. Glen will never get to have this again. No one will." I flip him onto his back and shove a pillow under his hips. He moves his hips, rocking forward, his pert ass sticking up in the air like a beautiful offering.

"Jace," he cries. "Please."

"Don't worry, baby. I'll take care of you. I'll always take care of you." I hold on to his hips, lining my cock up with his hole. I rub the head over his rim before pushing slowly inside. Once I'm halfway, I hold myself still, and pull out before slamming back in.

His body shakes and I pull another moan from him when I increase my thrusts, hitting him in the spot that has him shining brighter than a star. I rotate my hips, lifting his to play with his cock. I kiss the back of his neck, driving in deeper while holding his body closer to mine. He comes into the pillow and I lose all control after him, filling his perfect hole that squeezes around my cock so well.

Our heavy panting fills the room and I turn us both onto our sides, stroking his chest as we both doze off.

Thirty-Two

JACE

My dad's email has me tossing my phone down in anger. How did he get my info so easily? Why won't he leave me the fuck alone? Doesn't he get that I'm no longer his damn son. I haven't been in a long time. I shut my eyes, sitting at my desk and picking up the phone again to read the email, hoping I was only seeing things before.

Son,

I know you're still angry with me and probably hate me, but I won't be able to move on until you hear my apology in person. I know it may be too late to reconcile our relationship but I'd like to try anyway. I was a shit father and person. I know I was. Please just meet me somewhere one time and I won't bother you again.

I start to respond and delete the message when I reach the end. He doesn't deserve to have me answer back. At least he knows what he was. He'll always be that person in my eyes too. Nothing he can do will ever change my view of him. Meeting up will do neither of us any good, and he's not someone I'll waste my time going back to Texas for.

I set the phone on the desk and push my chair back, eyeing a sleepy Nate. He hasn't moved in a long time, appearing so peaceful and delicate. I get up to cover him more with the blanket and press a kiss to his cheek. He doesn't so much as wiggle, his soft breathing filling the room.

I look back at the open space between the barn doors, staring at the dark. I walk toward it, needing to get my anger out—needing to point it in a direction that's nowhere near my brother. I close the doors behind me, slipping on the boots I left outside. Crickets chirp and my feet move across the grass as I surround myself with the breezy night.

When I see all lights are off in the house, I march toward the shed that's out past the woods. Anger still hot in my veins, I unlock the door and smile down at the sick prick on the floor.

He was a friend of my dad's. I remember they used to shoot pool together, but I didn't know he was involved in the same operation my dad was. In and out of prison, he's been spending his days at an illegal brothel and searching out his next victim to sell to the owner. I have big plans for him too. Oh, his day will come soon enough.

The man who goes by Leonard looks up at me with scared eyes, scooting back with a gag over his mouth and his limbs confined. I drag the red bandana down to his neck, seething. "Morning, precious."

"Fuck you," he spits.

"No thank you," I say, snatching a knife from the wall. "Since you've seen my face, I think it's best to go with my original plan."

"Which one is that?" His voice is hoarse.

"Removing those eyes so you'll no longer be good at your job."

"No," he begs.

"You know what?" I cock my head. "I think I'll take your tongue too."

I'm not a killer. At least no one has driven me far enough to be one yet, but what I do to these men is sometimes so much worse than death. And they deserve every bit of it. Grabbing him by his hair, I yank his head back and pull his tongue out of his mouth, holding it while dragging the blade down the center. He makes a wretched sound with his throat, blood squirting all over the painter's tarp underneath my feet as I press harder. I don't stop until the small piece of him is separated from his body.

The small light up above is bright enough for me to see the tears lining his cheeks.

"Jace." A soft voice comes from behind me and my blood goes cold. No. He was sleeping. One day is all it took. One day of me getting everything I wanted right before losing it forever.

I drop the knife, slowly turning around. Nate's eyes widen in horror and he looks from me to the guy on the floor.

"What . . . what is this?" he croaks, stepping back.

"I . . . I told you not to come here, didn't I? It's not because I didn't want you enough. It never was. It's because I didn't want you to see how I've been able to bypass the nightmares."

His breaths quicken and tears hit his cheeks. "I . . . this isn't you."

"Yes it is." I grab his hand and he tugs away, his eyes full of confusion. Where's the disgust and anger?

"You don't have to keep going this way. You can still let him go. You can still stop."

"If I stop, they'll keep going."

His eyes blink and he looks at me as if I've sprouted a second head. "What do you mean?"

"This man works for a large trafficking ring. He steals young men and women from their families. He takes away all their hopes and dreams."

"How many has there been?"

"Six. Maybe seven. Not enough, that's for sure. Where there's one man like this, there's many."

"If this is your way of trying to change the past, you're only falling back into it. This is a dangerous game you're playing. No one will care why you're doing it, they'll only see you as a threat to everyone around you. You don't want that. I don't want that."

"Are you asking me to stop?"

"If not for me then yourself. You're not only putting a mark on your back, you're putting one on everyone you love too." His words hit me like a bucket of ice. He's right. I don't know why I've never thought of that. I've been risking my family's lives all this time and for what, to feel better about myself?

"Okay, I'll stop. This will be the last time, I promise."

"Good." He sucks his teeth, turning around.

"Where are you going?"

"Back to Texas," he heaves. "You were right. I shouldn't have come here."

"Don't," I plead.

"I'm sorry." He sniffs, tugging at his arm and glancing back at me. "I don't think I can do this after all. I don't think . . . I'm sorry."

My heart sinks and I drop to my knees as I watch him leave, my world crumbling around me. He's finally seen me for the person others told him I was, and I showed him I'm exactly what they were all waiting for me to be.

Thirty-Three

NATE

My hands shake against the steering wheel as I sit in the parking lot of the airport, trying to wrap my brain around everything I saw. Trying to understand why I want to go back. Trying to understand why I love him as much as before and wasn't as disgusted as I should be.

He cut a man's tongue off—he was the man my dad warned me about. A sick feeling comes over me. Not because of what he did but because of how easily accepting of it I was. That man really did deserve what he got, and there's no doubt in my mind the others did too.

These are bad men. They hurt people. But did that give Jace the right to take justice into his own hands? I meant what I said about him risking his life. These men are dangerous. Some might want revenge after he lets them go. They might tell their other friends about what he's doing, and say whatever it takes to send them after him.

Worry rattles my heart in my chest. This is why he wanted me far away from him. He really was doing it for me. As I'm about to reverse the car and drive back to him, a cloth is held to my mouth, a pair of cold eyes watching mine in the mirror as everything starts to fade to black . . .

Thirty-Four

JACE

The picture coming through on my phone shakes me to my core. I was on my way home from dropping my last victim in a random corn field four hours away from where I live when my phone chimed. I waited until I stopped to get gas to open the message, my heart threatening to escape my chest when Nate's scared face takes up the screen. No. No No.

It's finally happened. My darkness has reached him and I might not be able to save him from being smothered by it.

Unknown number: Meet me at the address below if you want to see your brother alive again. You have twenty-four hours before I start cutting his skin from his bones.

My throat constricts, eyes seeing red as I drive to the location stated in the message. Driving way over the speed limit, I only stop to get gas, and I bypass every car who slows me down. More hours pass until I finally reach an older house standing alone on the corner of a dead-end road.

I park the car and get out, shoving a gun into the back of my pants as I slowly approach the weathered porch. The door pushes open easily at the touch of my hand and I enter the house, eyes roaming in every direction as I stay on high alert.

"Back here," a familiar voice says, and my heart shoots into my throat.

I make my way to a small light shining from a room and pause in the doorway, bile rising in my throat when I take in my dad's wicked smile.

"I knew I'd get you to see me eventually. I was just really hoping it wouldn't come to this. Then again, I think I could make a pretty penny off this one."

"What do you want?" I say through clenched teeth.

His face turns to stone and he lifts the hood from Nate's face. His eyes are closed and his moving chest is the only indication that he's still alive.

"According to some important friends of mine, there's a guy who's been after men who fit a certain criteria. I didn't want to believe at first when one of them mentioned the scars on your hands, but then I had you followed. With this one's help, I was able to track down your location and contact info."

"What do you mean, with his help?" My hackles rise. "Did you put a tracker on him? Did you bug his fucking house?"

"Not me, but someone who was able to get as close as you were. I gotta say, I was disgusted at first to find out you were fucking your own brother, but then I remembered how he and his dad weren't really anything to you. And I just know how much this will break your mom's little heart."

I focus on what he's saying, pulling all his words together. "Glen . . . He—"

"Actually his name is Devin, but yeah, he was definitely worth the money I paid him." He looks back at Nate and my fists ball at my sides when he sweeps a finger along his cheek.

"Don't touch him." I knew Glen had skeletons in his closet but I didn't think they'd be worse than mine. He was working for my dad all this time. I know I told Nate I'd stop and I will, right after I make Glen regret ever stepping foot into his life. Fucking piece of shit asshole.

"Oh, but he's so tempting. And like you, I'm finding it too hard to resist him."

"I still don't understand what you want."

"I know your secret. One call and I can have your whole perfect little family buried six feet under. Don't think I won't."

"What the fuck do you want?" My teeth rattle in my mouth at my raised voice.

He lifts his head, lips tilting in a mocking grin. "For you to work with me again. You were always so good at taking care of the visitors before they went to their new homes. You were made for this life."

"Never," I bite out. "I'll never help you again. Find someone else."

"I've tried. None of them can be trusted for long. Always wanting to test out the merchandise, but I know you only have eyes for this one so I don't have to worry about that with you."

"Fuck you." I press my teeth together so hard, I swear I hear them start to crack.

He lets out an annoyed breath and removes a knife from his pocket, pressing the sharp tip to Nate's throat. "Then I guess your pretty boyfriend will be the first one I kill, and I'll keep going until you change your mind."

He pierces Nate's skin and a drop of blood beads at the small wound. My heart stops and I feel like the ground is swallowing me whole.

"Stop," I shout. "I'll do what you want."

His smile is back and I can't wait to cut it from his face. "I'm glad you finally came to your senses. I think I'll hold on to this one a little longer, for insurance. At least until the first job is complete."

"What do you need me to do?"

"I'm not as young as I used to be. I don't pick up men the way I could before. You, on the other hand . . . I'm sure you fight them off daily. You got this one's attention after all."

"So you want me to do what? Bring you back some clueless guy?"

"Exactly. Blond with blue eyes to be exact. It's what the client requested."

My ears ring. I need him to hear what I want him to hear, to make him believe I'm really willing to go through with this. "And you'll let him go once the delivery is made?"

"Correct."

"You won't touch him at all during that time, you hear. Not so much as a single hair on his head."

"You have my word."

Yeah, because that's worth a lot. "Okay. When do you need me to do this by?"

"Tonight will be good."

"Tonight?" I claw at my jeans.

"Yeah. You know what they say, time is money, and I've already wasted enough of it thanks to you."

"Okay, tonight."

As I'm turning around, he says, "Don't do anything stupid either. I won't hesitate to mess up this pretty face."

My blood boils and I hold my composure. "I won't."

I leave the house, my heart screaming to go back, but if I do I'll blow everything. Keeping my cool the best I can, I sit in my car with my face in my hands until a random idea pops into my head. I lift my head, smiling at myself in the mirror. Yeah, I'll get him his blond twink. Or at least make him think that's what he's getting.

A text comes to my phone.

Unknown number: Deliver him here when you have him, and let me know when it's done.

Me: You got it.

Unknown number: I'll have Nate with me for the little exchange. I'm so happy we're working together again.

I slam my phone against the steering wheel, causing the screen to crack, and steady my breathing before playing my plan over in my head, going through all the steps that need to be made until I'm sure it's nearly bulletproof.

Don't worry Nate, I'm coming for you.

And when I have him again, I'll do whatever it takes to talk *him* into staying this time.

Thirty-Five

NATE

I get shoved through the door of a house I've never seen before, and my shoes squeak against the floor when I don't move fast enough for him.

"He might have actually pulled this off and you'll be his prize if everything goes well."

I've never seen this vile man in person before, and I could have gone my whole life without breathing the same air as him. He keeps answering the phone to some guy named Devin, asking whether my parents have suspected me missing yet.

How would this friend of his know? My heart is sick with worry when the worst scenarios play in my head.

"What are you making Jace do?" I ask, not sure I want to know the answer.

"You'll see soon enough."

I've hated this man from the moment I first knew he'd hurt Jace, and I hate him even more now for coming back into his life. Hasn't he caused enough damage? Did he ever even love his son?

This man wasn't a father. He was a fucking predator. Jace was nothing but a pawn in his game. He liked control, pulling the strings and making him do whatever he wanted. His stupid rules and snapping fingers no longer worked, though, so he used what he knew would. How'd he find out? Has he been following me all this time? Did I lead him back to his very first victim? Am I the one who placed the mark on Jace's back?"

He guides me to a room down a dark hallway and when I enter the doorway, my stomach sinks. A man with blond hair sits on the floor in nothing but his underwear with his hands tied behind his back and a blindfold over his eyes. A gag is shoved in his mouth and he makes muffled sounds, fighting against his confines.

What have you done, Jace? What have you done in order to save me?

"Look what we have here. Exactly what I asked for. Almost." He rocks his head from side to side. "A little more toned than I would have liked, but we can fix that with a little time." He tugs me beside the scared blond and lowers himself to the ground to tie my ankles back together. Turning back to the other man, he reaches for the cloth over his eyes. "Now to check out those eyes."

As he reveals the man's closed eyes, he squints, looking closer. "What the–" And his body twitches when a knife is plunged into his throat. His eyes widen and he tries to speak, but blood bubbles between his lips when Jace shoves the blade deeper.

Sirens blare in the background and Jace shoves his dad to his back before getting to his feet. He stands above him, waiting for his body to go still before rushing my way. As soon as he unties me, I jump into his arms, peppering kisses on his face.

Footsteps pound down the hall and lights flash at us. A cop points his gun at the body on the floor and then us. "Someone call 911?"

"Me," Jace says. "I tricked my dad into letting me near a phone long enough to do it."

"Your dad?"

"Yeah. He's the man dead on the floor. He was going to hurt him and sell me. He was recently released from prison, after he'd been charged with involvement in sex trafficking. He found me and wanted to make me pay for failing him." Jace's voice sounds weak, and the man in front of us talks into his radio as another person in uniform steps in checking Jace's dad's pulse.

"Let's get these guys checked out and get their reports written down," one guy says to the other as we're steered out of the house and led to an ambulance truck.

They take our statements and our parents show up, following us to the hospital where they stitch the wound on the back of my head. Jace holds my hand the whole time, and my mom doesn't say anything, leaning into my dad as they wait for me to be released.

When we get back to their house, Jace climbs into my bed with me, spooning me from behind. My Mom doesn't walk in on us this time. She doesn't stop him from sitting next to me on the couch the next day during family movie night either, and I like to think she finally realizes there's no keeping us apart. Dad doesn't even blink, and in some way I think he's known all along. Jace is my person and I'm his. No one will ever stand between us again.

Thirty-Six

JACE

Mom hugs Nate goodbye right after Dad smothers him in his arms. They both turn to me next, giving me the same treatment, but as I start to walk down the steps to follow Nate to the car, a hand grabs my wrist. I turn around and Mom is smiling at me with watering eyes. "I . . . I didn't want you to leave without telling you I love you and how proud of you I am."

I squeeze her hand, feeling like my fingers are locking around my heart instead. "Mom—"

"No, I need you to hear this. I was wrong to send you away. I know now that I was. I only . . ." She sobs, wiping at her eyes. "I only wanted to do what I thought was the right thing, but all I did was push you away."

"It's okay, Mom. Really. I get it."

"It's not. You two clearly love each other, and I had no right to interfere with it then so I won't now. I see how you look at him and he looks at you. I don't think either of you could have found anyone more right than you are for one another. Sure, the way it happened is a bit unorthodox, but life has a funny way of doing that sometimes."

"Thanks," I say, swallowing down emotion as I drag her into my arms.

"I'm sorry you didn't hear me say all these things when you needed it the most. I'm sorry I didn't see what I needed to see sooner." She pulls back from me, her eyes pointing down, and she takes my other hand.

"You're saying them now and that's what counts."

"I want you both here every holiday, okay? And any other time you feel like coming home. I want you to call me every week and I want . . . I want to know my son more."

"I want that too."

Sniffling, she hugs me again and returns to where my dad is standing to wave at us from the porch as we drive off. Nate holds my hand, leaning his head on my shoulder as I turn up the music and begin my long drive back to Missouri with the man of my dreams in tow. He loaded the trunk and back seat with everything he felt he couldn't live without, and plans on getting a Pod for the rest later. He hasn't decided whether he'll sell his house yet, but we both decided we'll take it one day at a time. His boss is fine with him doing video calls only in the meantime.

We stop for food several times, and eight hours into our drive Nate switches places and pulls me into a kiss as he slides into the car. "I can't wait to be back on the futon with you."

I laugh, sweeping hair from his face. "You're the only person who'd ever feel that way, that's for sure."

"And the only one who matters," he says, sounding so sure of himself as he pulls back onto the road.

"You should want better than sleeping in that smelly old barn."

"I want exactly what I'm getting." He tangles his fingers in mine.

"And what's that? A bad back and the possibility of waking up with a duck shitting on your chest in the morning?"

A soft chuckle escapes him and he shakes his head, bringing the back of my hand to his lips as he briefly looks into my eyes. "Fully getting to be a part of your world and everything that's you. Bringing me home is your way for me to be a part of it all and I'm lucky I get to be the only one."

"You call that luck and I call that karma you must owe somewhere." I shoot him a cheeky smile and he elbows me in the arm, facing the road.

"No, me having to suffer through your bad jokes is probably karma."

"And you planning all the ways you're going to decorate the barn when we get settled is no doubt mine."

We both laugh and I kiss his cheek, dragging his hand into my lap and knowing damn well that of the two of us, I'm the one who's lucky. I'll gladly have him turn my whole home orange if it means I get to be right there with him during it all. As long as it means I get to be with him.

Thirty-Seven

JACE

One month later

I sneak into bed behind Nate after my short shower. He turns around, rubbing his face into my neck. "You're home."

"I am."

"Did you do it?" He glances up at me, nervousness evident in his voice.

"I did." I kiss his forehead and he nods against me, lifting the covers higher on us.

"Good."

"I love you," I whisper.

"I love you too." He smiles into my chest, tossing a leg over mine. Feeling him against me helps my heart and brain settle. As I begin to drift, I think of how Glen—or Devin—must look right now after the cops barge into his house on an anonymous call, finding a man tied up in his trunk and evidence of all my crimes spread throughout his garage.

I fall asleep with a smile on my face, knowing he'll not only be taking the fall for me, but that there's enough there to guarantee he'll be going away for a long time. He wanted so badly to have what I had. Well, in a way, he got his wish, while I got to keep the best of it all for myself.

Epilogue

NATE

One year later

Jace jumps into the pond after me, making a large splash. I swim toward him, wrapping my arms around his waist and pressing my head to his chest. This is the best way to cool down after a long day on the farm. After quitting my job and moving to Missouri, I started a program where patients get to experience a setting outside the office, incorporating horses in the therapeutic process. It's called equine therapy, and I get something out of it too. So does Jace.

His nightmares are getting better. He's hurting himself less in his sleep and is waking up looking more free after a night of uninterrupted dreams. I want to keep giving him that, along with every part of my heart. I was scared at first when I saw him with a bloody knife in his hand, but even seeing it firsthand, I knew he wasn't what they described him as on the news.

He no longer has to worry about them looking for him either. Not when my lying, fake fiancé is facing time for his crimes. Instead of making him fully stop like I originally asked him to, I made him promise to be more careful, and he has been. This is how he gets rid of his guilt, and this is his way of making it up to all the people he feels he let down. Who am I to take that from him, and who am I to stop him from doing what the justice system won't do?

Whenever he starts to doubt himself, I take him in my arms to remind him. "You aren't the monster, they are." And I mean every word. When I look at him, I see him for what he really is. The man who puts others first, and the person who prevents other people from suffering the same fate he did. I see my whole world. I see mine.

He tilts my head back, eyes shining brightly down at me. He tugs on the strands of my hair, and our tongues link like two matching puzzle pieces, always fitting perfectly together no matter how much time has passed.

"You almost ready to get out?" he asks after breaking free from my lips.

"Yes, but only because I want you to show me another way to use the tractor."

"You've been thinking about that for a long time, haven't you?"

"I do have a lot more free time on my hands now that I work for myself and control my own schedule."

"Does that mean I get to show you alternative ways to use the four-wheeler too?"

"You can show me whatever you want, anytime you want."

"Are you just saying that because you really want me to fuck you on the tractor?" His lips twitch.

"I'm saying that because I'm yours."

"Yes, you are." He shoves a hand between my legs, rubbing over my erection. "Only mine."

"Always," I say, looking forward to proving my words to him.

Athor's note

Thanks so much for reading my book and thanks for all your support. I loved every minute of writing this book and I hope everyone who reads it enjoys these two as much as I did. I always love a good hard-earned HEA and these two definitely deserved one.

Want more from here?

Join my reader group here

My Amazon store

Made in United States
Troutdale, OR
03/07/2025